NO GUILT OF BLOODSHED

JOHN BALTISBERGER

Published by Death's Head Press,
an imprint of Dead Sky Publishing, LLC
Miami Beach, Florida
www.deadskypublishing.com

First U.S. Edition

Cover Art: Justin T. Coons
Edited and Copyedited by: Candace Nola

The "Splatter Western" logo designed
by K. Trap Jones

Book Layout: Lori Michelle
www.TheAuthorsAlley.com

ISBN 9781639511259

Jedidiah Mercer is the creation of Joe R. Lansdale and used here with his permission.

Salem Covington is the creation of Wile E. Young and used here with his permission.

Dedicated to Zach Rosenberg, Jack Zaientz, Maxwell Ian Gold, Maxwell Bauman, Josh Schlossberg, and Rabbi Steven Folberg

With Special thanks to Wile E. Young and Lisa Tone for helping this novel come together

CHAPTER ONE

BRODIE

Brodie, California, 1879

BRODIE, CALIFORNIA, was a prosperous boomtown. Hell, the only thing more prevalent than the gold that flowed out of the mines was the malice the townsfolk were steeped in. The town had been established only twenty years earlier and had gone from a mining camp to an immense center of commerce and industry. And industry bred misery. Thousands of miners went down into those mines each day, each hoping to strike it rich, to be the one man who found the vein that would change the course of their history forever. And wherever men gather, so, too, gathers sin. Bordellos and gambling houses and bars.

The main street of Brodie, California, stretched over one mile, with countless distractions offered at every glance. And if you grew bored with the mundane pleasures that everyday sin had to offer, you could always take a stroll to the northern part of town, to Chinatown and their whorehouses and opium dens. If you had a taste for poison, you were sure to find your fill. You could consume until your pockets were empty, but the poisons of opium, whiskey, women, and coin were unforgiving masters, and those that found their pockets empty soon took to the streets to find a way, *any* way, to refill them.

Some went further than that. Some dipped deep until

even the most exotic of pains and pleasures tasted like dust in their mouth. For them, there was only one solution. They found religion. Brodie had been founded by Protestants, though its constant influx of immigrants meant that there were people of every stripe. Churches were all over; Catholics, Orthodox, and several non-Christian buildings were allowed to stand and hold services north of town. There was even a synagogue . . . well, there had been a synagogue. But the religion that the truly lost and damned souls found wasn't held in any protestant church or Catholic chapel. Rather, the cross of the Greek Orthodox church stood above the door, the only remotely holy thing about the building.

Inside, the true masters of Brodie, California, lingered and held court. When the church had first opened its doors and begun to usher in a new era of decadence, not many had batted an eye—it was an odd church, after all, a strange cross. People were too busy living their lives to worry about what others did on a Sunday morning. But slowly, the Orthodox flock had grown. And it came about that one of the faithful was elected Sheriff. Then it seemed more and more of the city council were members of the new church. It was often said in Brodie that the only place with more gold than the hills was the collection plate at the Orthodox church. Bankers, the wealthy, and those who sought positions where they could control others, they were all part of the flock of Saint Cyprian of Antioch Orthodox Church. All were welcomed, but especially those who could grease the wheels that would catapult Brodie from being a mining boomtown to being the center of American life in the hands of the priest, Dragan Risti.

Now, whether the evil that existed in the church attracted evil men or simply corrupted otherwise decent men was a conversation that was muttered quietly in many of the bars of Brodie . . . when men thought they were clear of any deputies or enforcers. Those who muttered too loudly, who pointed out the strange occurrences or made too much of a fuss would disappear. Gone from their posts, their alleys, their beds. No one knew for sure where they went, but the rumors whispered ever quieter said they became honored guests during the Feast of Saint Cyprian.

The sun was low in the sky when the stranger strode into town. He wore a light long-sleeved linen shirt under a heavy leather vest and a pair of stiff looking denim pants that covered most of his boots. The black derby on his head covered a black and silver sephardi kippah and cast long shadows over his face, almost but not quite hiding his features. A worn and well-used Swiss 1872 revolver rested in a gun belt that hung low on his hips, and a Terek Cossack shashka was tucked into a scabbard that looped into the belt. It would have struck onlookers as odd had there not been so much else that arrested their attention. He wasn't overly tall, but he was powerfully built and had darker skin, making his ancestry hard to pin down. Beneath a tangle of black curls, he had brooding black eyes that had made plenty a maid forget her promise to papa to stay pure. His nose had once been patrician and regal, but the multiple breaks it had suffered and the lack of medical attention he had received left it crooked. His beard was short and neatly trimmed. He looked so clean and well-groomed it would have been tempting for men to mock the stranger as being womanly, but for the cold look in his eyes and ragged scar that started at his left temple and traveled down his face, tugging his lips into a permanent sneer. Danger came off the soldier in waves. And he was certainly a soldier—and officer—if the sabre he carried meant anything at all.

But even the scar, the dark skin, and the sword were all secondary to the stranger's companion. The mastiff stood half the height of the stranger and looked to be covered in cracked and dried mud. Bristled hairs stood out between the cracks. It walked with a bestial grace while giving the impression of jerky movements, even when standing still. When it did move, dried flakes of mud fell to the ground and it left black footprints where it stepped. The gray and black beast's eyes were a dull blue glow, like twin sapphires had been placed in the skull of a broken statue. The dusty grime on the dog's head was carved with Hebrew letters.

The stranger came to a halt at the edge of town and looked up at the signpost, his travel bag slung over one shoulder. The hound sat heavily, looking up as its master spoke.

"This is it. He's here."

CHAPTER TWO
JOURNEY WEST

5 Months Ago

A UKRAINIAN PRISON, even in a small town like Ostropol, made you dream of being in the fires of Christian Hell. The icy fingers of the outside world intruded through every brick and saturated the bones in your body as surely as the iron bars kept you inside. There was no fire burning in the single room jail. No source of warmth. Four cages, not even worthy of the name cells, sat in the corners of the jail. Each was occupied, though only one occupant still breathed.

In the northwest corner, Josyp Artemenko sat rotting where he had bled out after tearing into his own wrists to escape the hunger and the cold. Caddy-corner to him, to the southeast, old Orest Ulyenko had finally died of his untreated wounds, wounds he had sustained trying to resist arrest for stealing bread. A thief had no place in life according to the Russians who ruled over the population of Ukraine. The third corpse, that of Yitzak, had finally let out his death rattle this morning. The blackened fingers protruding from the blanket were the only sign there was anyone there or what had taken him. To die of exposure while sitting in a building was an intense insult, a cruelty that seemed perfectly suited to the Orthodox guards who had chased him from Odessa.

Malechai ben Palache, sitting in the center of his cell,

breathed into his hands and rubbed them together. Malechai was a soldier, a mercenary, a man who had earned his coin fighting in wars all over the damned country. Had it been weeks? It felt like years. He wondered if his brother had actually died this morning or if it had been centuries ago and they were both in Sheol. He mourned Yitzak, his younger brother, as he mourned the death of every Jew who had been hunted down and butchered in the streets of Odessa, with a rage that simmered in his heart. It burned like the hot blood of his family had as it poured steaming over the cobblestones of the synagogue. It had powered him to fight back. With hot iron firing in one hand and the cold steel of the sabre in the other, he and his brother Yitzak had fought the Christians away from the doors. That fire had turned to ice. Jews killing Christians would only lead to more Jewish death, so they'd fled, hoping to draw away the rage and give them a target for chase.

It hadn't worked.

Now looking at his brother's dead hand, reaching up from the threadbare blanket as though begging for succor, for support, for vengeance, the fire was back. Every few days, the guards would make an appearance and drop some food into their cells—moldy bread, gnawed on bones, and desiccated uncooked vegetables. He would wait. He would survive long enough to grab the guard and pull him close enough to tear out one last Russian's throat before he succumbed to the elements himself. He would bring the fires of their hell with him until he at last went to meet HaShem.

There he sat, thoughts of revenge and murder keeping him as warm as he could possibly be, when his blood-soaked daydreams were interrupted by a scream from outside, the sound of pistols being fired, and soldiers running into the jail to get away from whatever was happening outside. They were shouting in Russian, moving as far from the door as they could get, reloading or just pointing their calvary swords and trembling. As curious as Mal was about what was causing all the ruckus, he wasn't one to ignore a gift. He reached through the bars and grabbed the hilt of a saber from the hip of a soldier. He pulled it out and slid it through the back of the soldier's neck in one smooth motion, delighting in the way the flesh parted so easily under the blade. He was about to turn to see who else he could reach when the doors of the little jail exploded inward.

The thing that came in looked like a massive dog, but it was wrong. The snout was short and stubby, and the gray and black hairs stuck out in opposing, unnatural directions beneath plates of baked clay. Its legs were more muscular than any wolf or dog Mal had ever seen. The soldiers reacted with terror and fired bullets at the canine, but they didn't seem to have any effect on the beast. Its blue eyes glowing in the gloom of the prison, it launched itself into the soldiers, gripping one by the leg and rolling like a crocodile, ripping the leg off with a sickening tearing sound. The screams were so loud that Mal thought his ears might burst. It reminded him of the night their community had been attacked. He had no pity. He reached through the bars again, swinging the sword at another soldier. But the angle was bad, and instead of decapitating the man, the sword stuck into the spine and refused to come loose. The soldier, his head loose and swinging nearly free, shit himself as he collapsed in a messy pile, taking the blade with him.

Mal turned to look at the carnage wrought by the beast. It sat in the middle of the jail, surrounded by the torn and dismembered limbs of the dead and dying. Mal smiled, the nasty scar on his face turning it into a cruel smirk. Now that the beast was still, he could see the word "TRUTH" carved in Hebrew letters in its head. The beast jerked its head to the side. Mal wrapped the wormy blanket around his shoulder and covered his face with the thin material, as much to stave off the cold as to protect his flesh from what came next. He pressed himself to the side of his cell, as far away from the wall as possible.

The explosion was sudden but expected. The cannonball blasted through the wall of the jail, struck the door of the cell, and blew it off its hinges.

Mal slowly lowered his makeshift shield and stared at the cannonball. A few feet to the right and he would be deader than the guards. At least some of them were still gasping for breath. The monstrous canine huffed at him and turned, walking out of the jail like he was bored now that everyone was dead. Hell, maybe it was bored. Mal wasn't. He turned towards the hole in the wall and growled.

"Goddammit, Ivanna," he called in Yiddish. *"Do you want to kill me or save me?"* He couldn't see his sister through the smoke hanging in the air, but there was no one else who would be so reckless. He pulled himself through the damaged wall and stood, a free man once more. As he had suspected, his sister stood only a few meters away, next to a still smoking cannon.

"Same difference to me, Malechai. Where is Yitzak?" His sister was a fierce demon who was just as prone to stab a man as talk to him. She wore a white dress that hung off the shoulders, her black hair tied up, showing off her supple neck, likely the bait she had used to get close enough to the jail to start killing. She watched Malechai's fist clench in anger and understood immediately. *"I swear they will all pay. Dearly."*

"They can pay later, when we get me some real clothes and to safety." He paused as the terrible mastiff rounded the corner of the jail and trotted up towards them. *"What the fuck is that thing?"*

Ivanna glanced at the monstrous dog and smiled a little, her blood thirst outweighing her sorrow at losing a brother. *"Him? This is Mishpat,"* the Hebrew word for judgement. *"He's on loan."*

"On loan? From where is he on loan, Abaddon?"

"Prague. Come, I'll explain when we get to the synagogue."

Walking through the country night beside his vengeful sister and what appeared to be a hellhound wasn't the most fun one could have in the Ukraine, but it was a far cry better than rotting to death alongside his brother in the jail. They had argued for a few minutes; Ivanna wanted to go immediately, but Malechai insisted they bury Yitzak first. Ivanna wasn't religious; she didn't care about spirits or rituals or propriety. She barely believed in modesty. Despite her protests, Malechai found a shovel and gave his brother a proper burial—well, as proper as it could be under the circumstances. In many ways, Yitzak had always been the odd one out. Ivanna was violent, passionate, as prone to start a fight as find a man she considered worth bedding in any community they had found. Yitzak was gentle, a good fighter, but one whose moral compass made those tough decisions in a gun fight tougher. People usually assumed Mal was the middle ground. Even-tempered, religious, but without an ounce of compassion for his enemies, he seemed like the reasonable one. Right up until he wasn't.

The Palache siblings had made their names as mercenaries, hired muscle and killers. Yitzak had been the smart one; he could outmaneuver and out plan any enemy army. Ivanna was a fantastic assassin when she felt like she was being respected by her employers. But Mal? Mal was the killer. He was the one who snuck into enemy camps and skinned their general and put him on display. Mal was the one who tortured captives for information. Mal was the one who took their little group from mercenaries to war criminals.

That and their darker complexion had made them pariahs in most northern towns they visited. The rabbis couldn't stomach what they had done. They preached peace and keeping your heads down. But what had that gotten them? Massacred. Every goddamned time. Mal had seen it all over the continent. A Christian would scream that Jews had stolen her child, and then men would come with torches, pitchforks, and guns. More often than not, the kid was found playing in the forest the next day, and if they weren't . . . Mal had found more than one child's corpse in the basement of their own home.

Mal spat, his mind wandering on this latest atrocity that had landed him in prison and Yitzak in a shallow grave.

Ostropol's synagogue was on a hill that overlooked the town. The Palache siblings circled the town, ignoring the cold in favor of avoiding more guards or any conflict with local Christians or, worse, the Russians, who seemed to be permeating every town in the Ukraine. War was coming. War was always coming. But for Jews like Malechai and Ivanna, war had already come. Mal wondered at the building as they approached. It was old, old and beat up, but the lights were on, and even from a distance, he could see that it was busy. A hundred or so men in long black coats and black hats milled about. Inwardly, he groaned at the sight of them; he never got along with his more zealous and orthodox brethren.

When the siblings stepped into the light, a hush fell over the assembled men. They must strike quite a sight. Mal was drenched in blood and hardly dressed for the Ukrainian night. Ivanna was even worse, and the men quickly looked away lest they be distracted from HaShem by her bare shoulders or some bullshit. Mal had no respect for the false modesty of men who usually turned out to be perverts. Several of the old men fell back, startled as the unnatural mastiff Mishpat joined them. But one man didn't fall back. He didn't stare, or avoid staring, at the shape of Ivanna's breasts through her dress. He looked only at Malechai. Disappointment and despair were written plain on his features, and why wouldn't they be? He was Saul ben Yechi; he had been the head rabbi in Odessa. The master of a now dead congregation.

"Hello, Malechai." He didn't ask about Yitzak, his absence was as obvious as the reason for it.

Mal nodded to the man and glanced at Ivanna, who was walking forward.

She glanced back at him. *"Well, come, Malechai, no sense in being angry and chastised in the cold when we could do it in the warmth of shuul,"* she chided him before she headed inside the building herself, followed by the horrible hound. Mal stood in the cold for several moments, looking at the ultra-orthodox Chassidim between him and warmth. His stomach growled, twisting itself into a knot. While he could not stomach the judgmental looks of these cowards who venerated martyrdom above saving people, his need for food and warmth outweighed his pride, and he followed Ivanna inside.

Inside there was indeed food—warm stew, bread that wasn't days old, and cold beer. Malechai sat at a small table off to the side of the sanctuary and greedily devoured the morsels in front of him. He knew he would like as not be sick from eating too quickly on a shrunken stomach, but he didn't give two good goddamns. Across the table from him, Rebbe Saul and Ivanna sat watching him. Ivanna with amusement, Saul with barely hidden impatience. The dog-thing sat at his feet. Without thinking about it, Malechai tossed a bit of bread to the dog. It sniffed the bread curiously and then looked at Malechai with its strange blue eyes.

"Go ahead, eat."

It took no more instruction than that for the hound to wolf down the offered food. He heard Saul tsk his tongue in disapproval. Mal sighed and looked up, dipping his bread into the stew to soften it before he took another big bite, gesturing with his free hand.

"Malechai, your brother and you. You did good to try and protect us," Saul started.

"Fat lot of good it did? Now Yitzak is dead, your congregation is dead, and us lesser sons of bitches are all that is left." Saul winced at the accusation in Malechai's voice. *"It's possible if we weren't the only mother fuckers raising iron and steel, maybe, just maybe, more of us would be here."*

"You know that isn't who we are, Malechai."

"Yeah, maybe not, but maybe it is who you need to be." Malechai sat down his bread and lifted the mug of beer, looking down into the swirling remainder of the foam. *"Me and mine will be out of your hair 'fore long, Rebbe. No need to worry about my piss poor attitude."*

The rabbi and Ivanna exchanged a glance. He knew the look. Whatever they were about to propose, he wasn't going to like.

"It isn't that simple, Mal," Ivanna said.

"Like hell it isn't."

"Don't you want to know why your brother is dead?" Saul asked.

"My brother is dead because you and your congregation are fuckin' cowards." Mal snarled through grit teeth, the scar on his face catching the light and making him look somewhat demonic.

"Why did we need to be? Why were we attacked? Those are the questions we needed the answers to."

"You were attacked because they hate us. Wherever we go, greed, stupidity, they will always hate us, Rebbe. There's no great mystery to it. They hate us because we are different." Mal leaned back in his chair, exhausted, tired of all this bullshit.

"Malechai, this was different, this was . . . a diversion." Saul watched the change come over Malechai.

Malechai understood diversions, he understood what they implied. Whatever the terror of the pogrom was, it was a secondary goal, a happenstance of someone's intent. His brother was dead, hell dozens were dead, all for someone's callous plotting.

Saul saw that Malechai was on his hook. *"While they were chasing us out of town, while they were attacking us in our homes . . . All on the words of the Greek priest . . . while they plundered and raped and pillaged . . . Dragan broke into the synagogue; he stole something and fled."*

"The hell did you have worth stealing?" Mal snarled, his eyes dark and dangerous.

"A dybbuk box. A prison," Ivanna said. Before Mal could wave off such a ridiculous claim, she kept talking. *"A prison for mallikim. Dangerous, hateful mallikim in the hands of that . . . that man!"* She spat out the word man as though it disgusted her to even have it in her mouth. *"Don't be stupid, Mal; don't be stupider than usual. That hound next to you, Mishpat, he was made by Rabbi Leow."*

Malechai leaned back, examining the dog. This was the infamous Golem of Prague? This hound was the creature that had turned the tide of pogroms and blood libel, created by the Maharal in their darkest hour of need? *"I thought it was supposed to be man shaped."*

"It's whatever shape it needs to be, and now it needs to be a hunter." Saul leaned forward, his voice low and sad. *"Do you think that the people of Prague would send their most terrible and secret weapon if the need were not true? If the danger were not real?"*

Malechai looked between their two faces. Ivanna's was like an alabaster statue of a Jewish Venus, beautiful and terrible in her wrath. Saul looked sad and scared. *"So you want us to hunt down this priest, Dragan, and bring back the box. Fine."*

"Not us, just you, brother," Ivanna corrected.

"What? Why the hell would I leave you here?" he asked.

"Because I don't speak English, and I need to stay here to protect them from . . . " she trailed off, not wanting to voice the fear that more pogroms were coming their way.

Malechai nodded and leaned back, his appetite gone.

He was about to agree when he realized what she had said. *"Wait, English? Where the hell am I going?"* He looked between his sister and the rabbi, not liking the discomfort on their faces. Whatever they were about to say, they knew it would piss him off.

"America, Malechai. Dragan fled to California."

CHAPTER THREE

THE DEVIL AT THE CROSSROADS

MALECHAI WAS NOT a fan of Brodie. He hadn't even stepped foot in the fucking town yet, but he already hated it. It was crowded and noisy. It looked new but not in a new and shiny way. Back in Europe, everything was old and sturdy. Here, the wood and boards and rope made everything look like it was a facade for a traveling troupe of actors. It looked flimsy. He reached down and scritched Mishpat behind the ear. Mal didn't know if the golem appreciated it or not, but it acted like a dog, hard not to treat it like one. The crossroads where he stood on the hill overlooked the town perfectly. He could see the whole development stretched out before him. He considered how stupid that was. Give him a line of cannons and he could destroy the place.

It wasn't like America was free of war. Half the talk on the ship he had taken to America had been about how they had torn themselves apart just a few short years ago. And over some dumb shit too. It wasn't until they had gone through the Panama Canal and picked up actual Americans that the picture had grown clearer. Hate and fear. It was always hate and fear. Malechai had heard the story plenty in his time. It wasn't always colored folk, though more often than not it was. People wanted power. They wanted power over other people, and when those people looked different, like the Blacks or the savage natives of the land, or acted different like the Jews did, it made it easy to see them as property instead of as fellow men.

Malechai nodded to himself. Nothing new about the new world, just strung together huts of Christians doing what Christians always did.

He started walking down the hill but paused when he saw several people heading towards him, a couple of them of them on horseback. A horse would be good, let him travel faster. He had a suspicion that Mishpat wouldn't have any trouble keeping up. Casually, Malechai rested his hand on the stock of his revolver. Starting off his arrival in Brodie with a murder wasn't likely to make his visit any easier, and he started to rethink the idea of robbing the men. Instead, he stepped to the side of the road and waited for them to pass.

The three men came up beside Mal and stopped. They were agitated, drunk—he could smell the alcohol on their breath from where he stood. They sat there on their horses, who were pawing at the ground, staring at Mal. He looked back at them. They were rugged men, more used to sleeping under the moon and working in the sun than being indoors.

"You comin' to town, then, stranger?" one of the men asked.

If these men rank themselves by the size of their ridiculous hats, he must be the leader, Mal thought.

"I've got a mind to," he answered. His accent, something he carried from being taught English by a German soldier, caused them to look at each other in confusion.

"You know, from back there, I thought you was a colored. But up close, you Injun, boy?"

"Nah, Howie, lookit him, he's probably one of them darker skinned Chinamen." The men laughed at their newfound game of guessing the stranger's race.

"No, I am not from China." Mal shook his head, bemused. He kept a hand on Mishpat's head. He could feel the growl in the dog's chest, even if it wasn't audible yet.

"I met a family while back, brown like him, called themselves . . . " the third man, the smallest of the three, thought for a moment. "Called themselves Arabs. From some place between them Brits and Africa."

"Closer," Mal admitted. "I'm a Jew."

"A Jew!" The leader, Howie, laughed. "Ain't no fucking way. You don't look like no Jew I seen before, but, uh." He killed his laughter and pointed at Mal's hand, which was still resting on his gun. "Why don't you drop the iron and hand over whatever coin you got, maybe open up your little bag there, give us a peek. Consider it a good Christian deed. We need some supplies for our trip to Silver River."

Malechai smiled, a lopsided, hungry smile made all the more unnerving for the way the scar on his face pulled at his lips. He didn't speak as he looked at the three men. He only saw the one rifle resting in the lap of the leader, but that didn't mean there weren't other guns. The middle man chuckled and cleaned his nails with a nasty-looking bowie knife. Still, this wouldn't be difficult. He whistled, sudden, loud, sharp. Mishpat moved.

The dog went for the horse's throat, tearing and ripping. The suddenness of the attack stunned the rider, who couldn't react before he was thrown off by the panicked animal. Mishpat abandoned the dying horse and leapt onto the fallen man with a snarl and the crunch of bones. The sound of rending flesh soon mingled with screams and pleas. Mal had started moving as soon Mishpat had, dropping his bag, and without pause or hesitation, he blew the lead rider's brains out the back of his skull. The rider's hat landed on the ground, still smoking from the hot lead that had cooked the brain as it passed through. Mal reached up, placing a hand on the horse's neck, patting it and calming it before it could panic as the rider toppled off.

"Howie!" The last rider had gotten off his horse to try to save his friend but turned when he heard the shot.

Malechai only needed one horse, and he needed none

of the men. Mal swept forward, holstering his gun, and grabbed the man's wrist in one hand. "I don't want to pay your toll," he said calmly, then grabbed the large knife the rider had kept in his belt and slammed it through his forearm, angling it to stick between the radius and ulna, and into the flank of the horse. The man screamed as the horse took off in a panic, taking the half-crucified man with him, screaming into the evening.

There was a near silence, the only sound coming from Mishpat tearing and chewing the flesh off the man it had killed. Most of the face was gone, the naked eyes staring up into the sky, the fear still writ plain on the dead orbs. Malechai shrugged and moved to search the dead leader. He rather liked the long coat the man was wearing, figuring it would protect him from the unrelenting sun he had heard so much about. He was bent over the man, pulling him out of the coat, when he heard the low growl of warning from Mishpat. He whirled around, his pistol at the ready, but saw nothing at first.

"It isn't polite to take things that don't belong to you."

The voice was succulent and alluring, like silk at night and honey drizzled over fruit. It came from behind him. He turned again, extending his gun towards the new figure. And goddamn, what a figure!

The woman in front of him, outlined by the setting sun, had a body he had only seen before in cartoons drawn by lonely soldiers in camps. Her wide legs were hidden by a long skirt that hugged the shape of her wide hips perfectly. Her waist was a slender thing, with just the barest suggestion of caramel skin peeking out between her bodice and the skirt. The bodice itself was tight, forcing her breasts up into two perfect mounds of flesh that made Malechai ache. Her neck was slender and almost called out to be caressed, kissed, bitten. Her face was ringed in black hair that fell about her face in loose waves. But goddamn, that face!

Large almond eyes with dark, smoky kohl makeup that just enhanced the smoldering blackness of her eyes, a pert nose slightly upturned, almost making her look like a doll. And the lips, goddamn, those lips! Malechai couldn't rightfully remember ever seeing lips so full and pouty as those. They were painted a dark cherry red that even in the darkness of twilight complimented her caramel skin beautifully. All of that beauty set on a slender face with high cheekbones.

For a moment, he was wordless. It wasn't until she cleared her throat and glanced pointedly at the pistol pointed at her that he realized he had been staring agape.

"Sorry, ma'am," he said, lowering the gun and holstering it. "However, I don't believe this man needs this coat anymore." He finally addressed her statement and went back to pulling the coat free, as much to keep his eyes off the woman as anything.

"Not what I'm talking about. They stole from me; their lives were mine to take." She said it flatly, no humor or joke in her tone.

Malechai freed the jacket, ignoring her, and slipped it on. It was a little tight in the armpits but not too bad.

She spoke again when he turned towards the horse. "Which means you done stole from me too."

Malechai paused and glanced over his shoulder at the woman. She had a small pistol aimed at him. He judged the distance, the lack of tremors in her hand, and the caliber of the weapon. She may miss, he might survive the shot, and he may be able to draw and down her before she could finish him. He turned towards her fully and put a hand on the horse's flank in a reassuring pat. In his side vision, he saw Mishpat circling around the woman, ready to pounce and tear.

"Well, for that, I am truly sorry. Nothing I can do about that now, though." He gestured to the two dead bodies. "You can take whatever they took from you now, though; they don't have much chance at stopping you."

She put her hand on her wide hip, and Mal caught himself staring at the curve of her again. "But you took their deaths, and you need to pay for that." She lifted her gun, taking a few steps toward him. "Hard to do that if your hound tears my throat out, I would think." She lifted her other hand and stroked his chest.

"And how would you recommend I pay for that?" he asked, resisting the urge to touch her back. His hands remained at his sides, near the gun. He watched her lips turn up in a wicked smile as her eyes traveled over him.

"I can think of a few ways, but not here. A gentleman would start by offering me a ride back into town."

Malechai chuckled. She was dangerous, going from pointing a gun to suggesting a bed in the span of a couple of breaths. But that was his sort of dangerous, the sort of relationship he had cultivated his whole life. And each and every time he stood in the debris of the aftermath of those relationships, he promised himself he would settle down and look to less crazy women, women who were respectable. He glanced at the saddle and then back at her. There was always next time, he told himself.

"I think that is probably true. You can ride." He tossed his bag on the back of the horse before offering her a hand to help her into the saddle, and within a few minutes, they were off.

She rode side saddle easily, watching Malechai through hooded eyes, probably sizing him up. He kept his eyes forward. Was she a whore? Probably, judging by her outfit. That didn't bother him much; he had been a patron, a friend, and a lover of whores before. But women who sold themselves for coin usually had an ulterior motive, be that a vengeful procurer or some personal goal. One had to be careful.

Mishpat jogged alongside them. Now that she wasn't sneaking up on them or threatening to kill him, the golem seemed perfectly content with her presence. Malechai wondered about that as well—dogs and hounds always seemed a good judge of character. But Mishpat wasn't an actual dog; despite its name being judgment, who knew if the thing had any ounce of it in its skull? It was a hunter, and for the moment, she wasn't prey. That thought caused Malechai to smile—she could be, just not the sort that Mishpat would be interested in. He looked up at her.

"My name is Malechai, you can call me Mal." He paused, wondering if the American would take the cue to give her own name and then wondering if she was actually American at all.

She was silent for a long moment, seeming lost in thought, before she answered. "Agrat." She looked down at him and smiled a little, a bit of warmth devoid of the predatory look she had so far adopted in their interactions. "I'm Agrat."

"Pleasure to meet you, ma'am."

"Oh," her hungry grin returned. "You have no idea . . . yet."

The roads of Brodie were straightforward, like someone had built them on a grid. They lacked the haphazard placement of Europe's cities, which had grown organically over the course of centuries. Malechai couldn't remember ever being in a place so young. But even the nice, neat rows of buildings and the hard-packed dirt of the road, so much smoother than jagged broken bricks, couldn't hide the wrongness in the air. It felt oppressive. Like the giant fingers of some terrible nephilim had curled over the town and were crushing the life out of it. Mishpat growled, keeping its body low against the ground; it felt the terrible shadow that sat over the town too.

Malechai glanced at Agrat, enjoying the silhouette she cast against the sky.

"You been here long?" he asked.

"Little under a year, I suppose. I came here with my family." Her voice was a hypnotic lilt that threatened to drown him in a daydream of whispering silks and forbidden caresses. "Here, this is my abode." She nodded to a building with the word *Saloon* hanging over the door. While he didn't know the word, he recognized the smell and look of the building; this was a bar. Outside, an older fellow tipped his hat at their approach. She slipped off the horse, taking the reins from Malechai, her fingers brushing his as she did. She moved to the man and handed him the reins.

"Ma'am?"

"This is Mr. Palache's horse. Get it stabled and make sure it's cared for."

Malechai watched as the man stood and took the horse around the back of the building, presumably to the stables. *"Mishpat, stay with the horse,"* he said in Yiddish.

The golem looked at him, letting out a small whine in argument.

"Guard outside. Make sure no one gets the drop on me."

Mishpat gave a bark—it sounded like a bark, but it filled the air with unwholesome reverberations—and then turned to follow the man and horse out back.

Agrat raised an eyebrow at him.

"Dog likes to sleep outside. I like to sleep indoors, preferably in a bed."

Agrat's face broke into a mischievous smile, and she pointed to a nearby building. "Oh, well, that there's a bunkhouse. I'm sure they have plenty of empty beds."

"And that's where you would like for me to go?" he asked. "I seem to remember I needed to repay you for my transgression."

She feigned a look of surprise, her mouth forming a little *O* before she pursed her luscious lips as if deep in thought. "That's right, you owe me. I suppose you'll just need to come upstairs so we can think of something." Her dark eyes glittered in the lamplight of the street, and without another word, she took his hand and led him inside, past the bar and up the stairs to the room she called her own.

As soon as the door closed behind him, he dropped his bag and wrapped his arms around her waist and pulled her close, his lips hungrily finding hers like a man starving. She laughed at his manhandling and met his lips with a deep moan of satisfaction. She ran her fingers up his face, pushing his hat off his head as she answered his hunger with her own. He melted into her lips; they were as soft as they had looked and tasted like brown sugar, sweet with a hint of spice. When they broke the kiss, she pulled back from him, her fingers hooked in his vest. Then she roughly shoved the dead man's coat off his shoulders.

"Mighty presumptuous of you, Mr. Malechai," she said with a wicked grin, running her fingers over the leather of the vest before she deftly began undoing the buttons and working the vest off.

He dropped his arms, working to kick off his boots, distracted by the way she kept darting in to plant soft, warm kisses on his face. In the back of his mind, he tried to remember the last time a working girl had been affectionate. He couldn't. But it was nice. It felt like he was wanted, desired. He finally managed to get his boots off just as she gave up on his shirt and ripped it open. She immediately attacked his chest with her mouth, her tongue gently gliding along the skin, her teeth catching his skin in playful tugs. He reached around her and worked on the lace binds of her bodice with quick, practiced fingers. She laughed, delighted, when he pulled the constricting garment away from her and stepped back, his hands on her narrow waist to admire her body.

Her skin was soft and warm, the small waist coming up from wide, well-defined hips, and he could see the muscles moving just under the skin of her stomach as she wriggled in his hands. Each of her round, full breasts, heavy in his hands as he ran them up her body to explore, was tipped with a dark brown nipple that hardened under his thumbs. He leaned forward, licking and kissing. She gasped a little at the roughness of his beard and the warmth of his mouth on her breast as he explored her as eagerly as she had done him.

She pulled back, ignoring his grunt of protest, and pulled him to follow her with a finger in his waistband. She led him towards her bed and pirouetted to put his back to the mattress, then shoved him down onto it. As soon as his ass hit the mattress, she was on her knees between his legs, her skirt billowing out around her as her hands moved to his belt.

"Oh, looks like you're ready to make good on your debt," she said as she ran a hand over the shape of his hardness through his pants before returning to getting those pesky pants off.

"I aim to please," he replied, lifting his ass off the bed to allow her to slide his pants down.

She reached up, giving his shaft a few strokes, her dark eyes alight with lust and approval.

"Oh, I think you ought to be able to, Mr. Malechai." And without further word, maintaining eye contact, she leaned forward and took him between her lips. A deep moan in her throat reverberated up his shaft.

Malechai leaned back, the warmth and smoothness of her mouth almost painfully good. He concentrated on the feelings shooting through his body as her head bobbed, her tongue coiling around him like a serpent. He felt his breath quickening almost immediately. The sensations she was causing were almost too much for him to stand. He felt himself getting weak, as if all of his strength was being drained from him through his cock.

Malechai's eyes widened, and he grabbed the revolver from the holster of his belt and pressed the barrel to Agrat's forehead, his eyes narrowing.

"That's enough, I think."

Agrat opened her eyes and looked at the gun with his manhood still in her mouth. She didn't look scared, just annoyed as she pulled back, her too long tongue dragging along the underside of his cock and almost bringing him to orgasm. He winced at the intense pleasure, but the gun never wavered. She licked her lips and rose. Stepping back, she watched him with cruel amusement.

"Was I not good?" Agrat asked in Russian.

"Succubus," he responded in English, refusing to play her game. "Trying to steal my soul, my strength. You would take me and then leave my withered husk to feed the buzzards." He reached to pull up his pants with his free hand but stopped as her hands went to the tie on the side of her skirt, which was keeping it up. His body responded to her even as he kept the gun trained on her.

"I don't want your soul, Mal, and I don't need your strength. I have my own." She spat that out and glanced up at him, her eyes angry and demeaning. For an inhuman creature, she looked much like any angry human woman. "I just wanted to enjoy myself." She continued working on the tie, and her skirts fell away.

His eyes darted down; her hips and belly made him ache with need. She smelled like cinnamon, and her sex called to him, causing his body to tremble. Her legs were human through her powerful thighs, and then below her knees he could see red scales, reptilian legs that ended in clawed talons.

His eyes shot back up to her face. Any other woman and a man would be horrified by the legs, or hypnotized by her breasts, or the play of hardness and softness her muscles caused in the shifting light of the room. But Agrat's face was just as alluring, and just as terrifying, as any other part of her.

"Right, and then feed me to your kin from the box you escaped from." He snorted.

In a heartbeat, she was on him. She straddled his lap, one hand on his throat, choking him, the rage in her eyes causing the dark eyes to glow like molten lead. "They are not my kin, Palache. They are slavers. They treat me like a whore and a thing to be traded!" Her teeth were sharp, sharp enough to tear out his throat.

He pushed the gun under her chin and pulled the hammer of his revolver back . . . and then froze as he felt her hand on his shaft, guiding him to her entrance.

She pushed down with her hips, enveloping him and pulling him into her. He shouted, both in shock and pleasure. She gasped, her hand still on his throat, though she wasn't squeezing as hard anymore.

"I just want to kill the priest and get the box," Malechai said, his free hand going back to support his weight as he rocked his hips against her.

She moaned, her lips opening in a gasp of pleasure as she rode him.

"Stop . . . the demons." He begged his body to pull the trigger, but he couldn't bring himself to do it—and it had nothing to do with her nails grazing his throat.

"Then kill the priest, get the box, kill the mallikim. I am no threat to you." She yelped as he rose in a thrust to meet her hips, her head whipping back. When she rolled her head forward, she was flushed, her voice coming out in short gasps. "I'll help. I'll help you."

And then she came down again and began rocking her hips back and forth. The effect was almost immediate, and he felt his control slipping.

If he was going to shoot, he had to do it now. But the gun slipped out of his hands, and he found her body, squeezing, stroking, touching . . . he bucked under her, shooting his seed into her as he pulled her close and buried his head in her chest. She rode him through their mutual orgasms before letting go and letting him fall back onto the bed.

"A deal. I'll make you a deal." She panted, her hair plastered to her face and shoulders with sweat.

"What deal?" Mal expected to feel guilt or disgust—for her and for himself. He expected to feel drained, to feel his heart give out, or at least feel weak. But he didn't. He felt the warm afterglow of an amazing fuck. He stared up at her, feeling her muscles twitching around him, the subtle aftershocks of a good orgasm.

She slowly laid on top of him and rolled off to the side, whimpering as he fell out of her. "Like your king David made with Saul."

He looked over at her; she was lying on his arm. His gun was somewhere, on the floor probably, and he wouldn't be able to get to it before she killed him, if that's what she chose. "David and Saul? You want me to marry your daughter?"

"The other part of the deal, genius." She propped herself up on an elbow, running fingernails over his chest in slow, lazy circles. She laughed at his look of bewilderment, an honest laugh, no mockery or cruelty in it. And Mal struggled to understand this creature. "Saul asked David for one hundred Philistine foreskins in exchange for his daughter. I am asking for one hundred foreskins from those who serve and follow the mallikim."

"In exchange for?" He decided not to ask what she wanted the foreskins for.

"I'm not enough?" she asked, archly raising an eyebrow.

"Enough for that trade, sure, but you said for help. Fucking you isn't going to help me kill the priest."

"Charmer," she said before rising and moving to a nearby table to pour a couple of glasses of whiskey. She offered him one. He took it and watched her drink before drinking his own.

"I wasn't lying. I don't need your strength; I have my own. The stories about my kind are warped through the lips of men desperate to be important and wanted. I have the strength of every woman who has been used unkindly. I have the strength of the subjugated. If you deliver my price, I will grant you that strength, for a time."

Malechai thought about that for a moment before nodding. "I think I can live with those terms." He would need to kill a lot of people, but it was likely that a lot of people would need killing. And maybe it was an ill or evil power, but he was no saint. He had no reason to play nice or by the rules. It was the priest's fault his brother was dead, and as far as he was concerned, the people of Brodie in league with the priest were just as guilty. He rose and started to pull on his pants.

"And where are you going?" Agrat asked, bringing her cup to her mouth to hide her smirk.

"I figured you got what you wanted, said your piece. I'll head to the bunkhouse before I wear out my welcome," he responded, looking for his shirt.

"Well, I can't see the future, but I'm thinking we could wear out the bed before your welcome wore out." She sat on the bed, leaning back and arching her back so that her breasts thrust at him in invitation.

Bedding down with an infernal succubus while hunting a priest and murdering people in order to deliver a grisly prize to the demoness for her diabolic deal? He glanced at the door before pulling his pants down again. He was no saint.

CHAPTER FOUR
BLESSINGS BY THE MORNING SUN

MALECHAI EXTRACTED HIMSELF from under the succubus. His body ached in ways that he was sure he would be feeling for a week. He grabbed his pants and pulled them on as he moved to wash his face in her water basin, then stared at his reflection in the mirror. His body was covered in scars and welts, the receipts for a life of war and violence. Mixed in with all the damage were fresh scratches, bite marks, and dried-on lipstick. He licked his thumb and rubbed at one of the marks for a moment, working it out before he found and pulled on his shirt. It was shredded. No decent way to salvage it. He sighed and opened the small bag he had traveled with and dug around to pull out a battered set of *teffilim* and *tallit*. Silently, he stood at the small window and stared out as Brodie woke up. He wrapped the leather straps around his arm and then his head. Pulling the prayer shawl over his shoulders and head, he started his morning prayers.

Agrat rose halfway through his recitation of the *Amidah,* pulling the sheets up to cover herself. She watched with a small smirk but didn't interrupt and kept any snide remarks to herself.

Finally, he finished his prayers and began unwinding the *tefillim.*

"Faith never looked so good," she teased.

He chuckled in response but concentrated on getting the leather straps loosened.

"Morning prayers after what you did last night?" She clucked her tongue in false admonishment.

"I don't think the holy one gives two shits who you fuck; I think he cares about who you fuck over," he said, watching her rise and carry the sheet with her, hiding her body. He figured the modesty was just as strange as his morning prayers after the previous night.

"Oh, you're a regular philosopher, Mal." She stepped behind a room divider, and he listened to her shuffle around. After a moment, she threw a shirt over the divider to him. "See if this fits. It may be a little tight."

He pulled on the shirt and laid his tallit over it while slowly walking around the room, examining things now that he wasn't distracted. He had met strange beings on his travels before, monsters and witches and *sheydim;* but this room was surprisingly human. There were little knick-knacks and pictures, grooming supplies, a rifle in the corner. All things he would expect from any working woman's home. On the small table in the corner of the room, he found a map of the town.

"How recent is this?" he called.

Agrat appeared from behind the divider and approached him. She was in a much plainer outfit than last night. Her skirt was a creamy off-white linen, and she wore a conservative blouse—well, as conservative as her curves allowed any blouse to be. He stared at her. Even in clothes that showed nothing and left everything to the imagination, she was beyond mortal beauty. She glanced at him and blushed, and he wondered how long she had practiced blushing to make it seem natural. She was thousands of years old, a creature of seduction, and one who would gladly rip his soul out if he let down his guard.

"Fairly recent. I think there's some expansion out towards the mine, but other than that, fairly accurate. What's your plan?" she asked.

Mal didn't rightfully know. The truth was that Yitzak had been the planner, the brains of any operation. Mal had always been the muscle. He pointed at a little square that signified Saint Cyprian. "Suppose I'll head to the church and kill a priest."

Agrat rolled her eyes. "I didn't know I was sharing a bed with a simpleton. There ain't no way you'll get past the doors to the church."

"I can be pretty persuasive."

"Don't matter, you aren't more persuasive than magic wards," she said and then rolled her eyes at his questioning look. "Did you really come all the way to California without a lick of knowledge or foresight?" She stood straight, crossing her arms under her chest and giving him a pointed look.

"I got a plan: find the priest, get the box, kill the priest." He smirked at her exasperation. "Well, go on, tell me what I got to know to succeed."

"There are five wards, one for each of the most powerful mallikim and lillikim within the box, which protect the church from any who would do it, or its master, harm. You can either convince them to help you or break them to break the seals. Even then, it won't be easy. He has siphoned power from the box, a box that has held spirits since the time of Solomon. Which is why you'll need my power."

Malechai nodded, his fingers tracing over the map. "So I'll have to find these demons."

"You could just ask." She grabbed a small container of red rouge she had undoubtedly used for her lips and drew circles on the map. "Mammon manages the bank in the heart of town. Baladan oversees the mines. Tanin'iver serves as the local garrison's chef; I don't want to make any guesses as to what she serves the soldiers. And finally, Beliya'al has taken over the law, posing as a sheriff." She put her makeup away and stood back.

"Five," he said, looking at her. "You said there were five wards I would need to break."

"Well, I think we can agree you already showed some dominance over the first one," she answered with a sly grin.

Mal cleared his throat but smiled at the teasing. "All right, what about these other areas? Do I got any potential allies against this motherfucker?"

She pointed to the north. "Up here is Chinatown; they've mostly warded the area against demons using their own magic. Then somewhere on the outskirts of town, you'll find the Paiute natives. Other than that . . . " She shook her head.

"What about Jews? Can't tell me I'm the only Jew in Brodie."

"No . . . but they won't be much help. Ever since the sheriff and his deputies burned down the synagogue, the Jews have hidden in their homes." She paused, seeing the dangerous fire in Malechai's eyes. "If they try to leave, they're shot down by Risti's men. So they hide in their homes and wait to starve."

She was fanning the fire of hate and vengeance in him. Maybe she was manipulating him, maybe she was trying to spur him on to greater acts of violence and cruelty. But if so, that didn't require much prodding.

"Where?" he asked.

"The guards posted outside their homes won't hesitate to kill you."

"Where?" he repeated.

"And they know the layout of the town. They'll corner you."

"Stop stalling, Agrat. You told me for a reason; now just tell me where."

"The Jewish part of town is in the southwest corner near the shops." Agrat frowned and walked over to her bed and plopped down, watching him. "Those shops have mostly been taken over by members of Risti's church."

Malechai nodded and pulled on the dead man's coat before kneeling next to his bag and lifting out a small wooden box filled with spare cartridges. He opened it, making sure no moisture had gotten into the box before shoving it into the coat's pocket. He would need a few other things before he was really ready to take on the whole of Brodie and its demonic masters. "Where abouts is the general store?" he asked.

"Why? What do you need to get?" she asked, confused by the seeming non sequitur nature of his question. When he answered her, she laughed, loudly and honestly.

Malechai stood at the counter of the general store, looking over the selection of knives on display. The shopkeeper was staring at the hound that accompanied Malechai. Mal needed a good knife, a knife that was sharp and had a heavy enough back to aid in chopping.

"Uh, sir?" The shopkeeper, a nervous-looking man with a graying mustache, interrupted his thoughts. "If you could, leave your animal outside, we . . . we don't allow . . . " He searched for what to call the mastiff shaped monstrosity. "Uh, well, that is to say, we don't allow animals inside," he finished lamely, looking at another man who was watching the entire exchange silently. The other man was burly and sat with his arms crossed over his chest—protection for the shop, one could assume.

Malechai looked between the burly man who was watching them to the shopkeeper, meeting his eyes, his look just as dangerous as Mishpat's. "You don't like dogs?" he asked.

"Well, it isn't that, it's just that . . . "

"No, you don't like dogs. I understand, but Mishpat is a good boy." His hand fell, and he stroked the dog's head. Mishpat, playing the part, looked up at Mal and licked his hand, his heavy tail giving two wags that thudded against the floor of the store. Malechai looked back at the shopkeeper, so did Mishpat, with a warning growl in his throat. "So, I'll take this knife here." He tapped the case over the large bowie knife. "That and the sack, and me and my dog will go."

The burly man uncrossed his arms and pushed himself up. He walked towards them as the shopkeeper opened the case to retrieve the knife. When he spoke, his voice was like gravel. "What do you need a knife for when you got that fancy sword at your hip? I assume you got that in the service. Do they not teach you how to use it? Just for show?"

Malechai turned to face the man, and an ugly smile broke across his face. He used to have a nice smile before the disfiguring scar. "The sword is designed for killing people." Malechai took the knife from the shopkeeper's outstretched hand and turned it, looking at his reflection in the polished steel. "This . . . is for snakes." He reached into his pocket, not taking his eyes off the burly man, as if daring him to object. He pulled out a silver coin and tossed it to the counter. "It is not minted here but should be worth its weight in silver. Good?" he asked.

After quickly weighing the coin, the shopkeeper nodded. "That will be fine, mister."

Mal tucked the knife into his belt and grabbed the burlap sack, slinging it over his shoulder. He winked at the burly man and turned towards the door.

"Time to go kill some snakes."

Myles Duncan spat out a wad of tobacco and stared off into space. This was all bullshit, far as he was concerned. Wasn't sure why so much effort had to be spent keeping these Christ-Killers holed up in their houses. If it were up to him, he woulda just run 'em all outta town. But the Padre wanted them to suffer, didn't just want 'em gone, wanted them dead. And not just dead but suffering. Myles sighed and glanced around the little square in the middle of the small community. The shutters were all drawn closed, hiding the Jews that stood inside saying their weird prayers in their weird language.

Myles had seen enough in Brodie to know that strange happenings were afoot. The Padre could summon angels and craft miracles. Any man of god able to bring forth power like that ought to be heeded. He glanced at the burnt-out husk of the Jewish church. The embers that remained from the blaze still smoked. They hadn't even removed the bodies yet. At least it didn't smell like cooking meat anymore. That had been upsetting. Not because it had smelled bad, no, it had smelled *good*. It had made Myles's mouth water and his stomach rumble. He was no cannibal, but goddamn, did the smell of cooking Jews just set his hunger on edge.

Somewhere in those cinders and fallen planks was their priest, still clutching that weird scroll they worshiped. Myles had to admit he didn't understand the Jews, but then again, he didn't have to understand them; all he needed to do was make sure none of them left their houses without getting a belly full of buckshot. Myles didn't think they needed five men to guard this little community; hell, it could probably be done with one man if that man were quick enough with a gun. But Myles would be damned if he complained. He was being paid good money to stand around doing nothing all day. The opportunity to kill some people guilt free wasn't a bad perk either.

He adjusted his stance. He needed to take a piss. He was taking a lot of pisses these days, and it burned. A side effect of visiting the girls of Lola's Goat, the bar closer to the route the miners took home. Sure, Lola's girls were a bit more than "gently used," but goddamn, did they know some tricks that would make a whore anywhere else blush. He grinned at the memory of taking a piss in that one girl's face before getting going. There was just something about degrading women that felt good, felt natural to him. He adjusted his cock; it was twitching at the memory. Of course, that burned too. The foreskin pulling at the head was like fire against the inflamed and infected skin. He sighed and tugged at his crotch. He caught the eye of Rebus, who was standing guard across the way, and he waved, trying to signal that he was going for a piss.

After Rebus waved back, Myles made his way down the alley and stretched. Pulling his pants down, he grabbed his cock and flopped it around for a moment, peeling back the crusted foreskin to examine his engorged head. It looked mad and was leaking a mealy yellow liquid. It stank like hell. Myles gagged a little and lifted his head to get clear of the odor wafting from his own penis. He sighed and, keeping his head up and turned away, pissed against the scorched base boards of the synagogue.

Myles felt something cold on his balls. He looked down and froze. The stream of reddish tinged piss trickled to a stop as he stared at the seemingly massive blade of the knife tucked firmly under his balls.

"If you scream, I cut." The voice in his ear was rough, heavily accented, and exceptionally dangerous. Myles tried to look at him without turning his head. All he saw was a scar that stretched a mouth into a snarl.

"How many of you are keeping my people here?" the voice asked.

Myles shuffled, but stopped when he felt the blade pressing closer. He considered lying, he considered throwing an elbow. He also considered not having an inch to his name. "F-five," he stuttered. "I mean, four after me, but I'll leave, I'll get out of here, and you won't have to worry about me none. In fact, I—"

Myles was interrupted as the stranger snaked an arm around his neck and covered his mouth, jerking his knife hand up as he did. Myles stared down at the 2 inches that plopped to the gravel road like a dead fish, his balls jiggling there in the swiftly growing puddle of blood.

Myles screamed under the hand; he thrashed, but the stranger kept his vice-like grip.

"Shh, shhh," the stranger cooed in his ear. "That's one."

The knife came up, still slick with the blood that gushed out of his gaping cock-hole and slammed into and through his chin. Up through the pallet and into the brain.

Myles convulsed once, twice, and then shuddered, shitting himself as he died.

The stranger, still in his bowler and tallit, had expected that and had angled his body enough to not be shit on. He dropped the dead man and bent down to toss the severed dick into his burlap sack.

"If this is all you are packing, I understand why Agrat needs a hundred," he told the dead man. "No wonder you Goy do not circumcise, cut any off and it would be gone."

Malechai glanced down at the dead man and knelt to clean the blade on the man's shirt. Moving to the mouth of the alley, Mal took in the sights and the smells. Sure, the architecture was different—the buildings were built of wood and not stone—but a ghetto was a ghetto no matter how you sliced it. Mal stood in the shadows offered by the too-close buildings and marveled that the flames hadn't spread further. Big wooden city like this, they must have controlled the blaze, which meant that every part of this was purposeful. Not that he was one bit surprised. He had seen the gallows in the center of town as he had made his way here. Death was a spectacle in the American West. Murder was a game. Luckily, Mal was well versed in the rules of this particular pastime. He watched the guards who were visible. He had already made three of them. Well, two of them now that 'little pisser' back there was dead.

Mal stepped back from the mouth of the alleyway and looked around. When in doubt, get the high ground. Always, *always* take the high ground. Mal pulled himself on top of a nearby crate and jumped up, catching the lip of the roof he was next to and pulling himself up. He clambered onto the roof on his belly, sliding forward until he could safely rise to a kneeling position. There were the others. Two more men sitting on roofs. One was clearly asleep, an empty bottle on its side next to him. The other was flipping cards into a hat, oblivious to the world around him. Mal smiled grimly—this was almost too easy. Mal slipped across the roofs, staying low and approaching from the card flipper's blind spot. Easy to do when all the homes were built so close.

Mal hit the man's roof already running. The sound caused the card-flipper to look up, eyes wide in confusion that turned into fear. But by the time he opened his mouth to shout a warning, Mal was on top of him. Mal leapt up and brought his boot crashing down into the man's face, enjoying the crunch of bone and teeth as he landed, his full weight and momentum easily crushing into the skull. Bits of biological debris splortched across the roof. Mal stood there in the man's brain for a moment, waiting for his convulsions to end before he bent down, pulled down the man's pants, and sliced off his cock in one smooth motion. He dropped it into his sack. So far, so good. Mal glanced down the side of the roof and, satisfied, jumped down, catching himself on a window ledge to slow his descent.

There in the window was a young girl. She looked terrified; her long black hair hid her face as she trembled in fear.

"Hello," he said in Yiddish.

"Hello. What are you doing?" she asked, surprised that the strange sky-man spoke Yiddish.

"Oh, just hanging out, taking care of the bad men," he responded. *"Soon, it will be safe to come out,"* he promised her before dropping back down.

She leaned out the window to watch the strange man and gasped when the massive mastiff trotted up to him.

Mal waved at the little girl to go back inside before he knelt next to Mishpat. From here, he could see the two guards on the ground slowly walking their rounds. It was clear that all of these men thought they were untouchable, that they were something special. He would disabuse them of that notion. Mal pointed at the farthest guard. *"Fetch."*

Mishpat was off. An echoing, haunting howl loosed from the maw of the canine shaped monster that caused both men to turn in fear. Malechai waited until Mishpat had passed the first guard to follow. Both were distracted. Neither saw him rushing forward. Mishpat reached his target first. He grabbed the man by the genitals with a mouth that could swallow a cat whole. His teeth sank into the flesh of the man's ass and pelvis, and the man screamed in horrified pain. Mishpat lifted the man and swung him about, slamming him into the ground with every furious shake of his head. Even from his own approach and attack, Malechai could hear the ripping and tearing of flesh. The man died after the third shake, his broken neck rag-dolling around, and Mishpat worked to tear his prize free.

Seconds after Mishpat had grabbed the man, Malechai had reached the other guard and, without slowing down, rammed the bowie knife between his ribs. As soon as he felt the hilt guard hit bone, he withdrew and stabbed again on the other side, then stepped back. The man tried to scream out, cry for help, hell, maybe even cry for mercy. But his swiftly deflating lungs just didn't have the power to do it. Malechai tilted his head, watching the man trying to draw breath as he watched his friend get his balls chewed off by a monster. Life was rough all over. Mal knelt next to the man.

"I wouldn't worry about him; he's dead. You, you will be too, but it will take more time, be worse. I know you are probably thinking, how could it be worse? Than that?" Mal gestured at the mess of the man as Mishpat padded back to them and dropped the mutilated organ in at Mal's feet. "For you, it will be worse, because I'm going to take your skin, and I'm going to use it to tie up your drunken friend." Mal pointed the knife up at the building where the drunkard was still sleeping. "I'm going to use your intestines to make a tourniquet to staunch the blood, just to let him live a little longer. You see? Worse."

Not waiting for the answer that he knew he wouldn't be getting, Mal got to work.

Mal tied the end of the burlap sack as he stood over the drunkard. The man was still trying to scream around the long strip of hairy flesh that was tied around his mouth like a gag. His eyes were huge and focused on the slick shit filled intestines tied tightly around the base of his balls and the savage wound that was dribbling blood just beyond the knot. Mal scratched an itch with the knife, smearing his face with the man's blood while he looked over the town from his vantage point. The man had been so sound asleep that Mal had been able to kill all the other guards, come up here, tie the man up, and then sit and fashion a noose from some loose rope he had found in the alley.

"I know what you're thinking, friend," Mal finally said. He spoke softly, barely over the man's muffled whines and screams. Mal imitated a high falsetto voice. "Why me? I am a good Christian man; I don't deserve this!" He chuckled, kneeling next to the man. "No, you're not. You think because you follow a certain religion that the rules of decency don't apply to you. Your dead god gave you permission to be an asshole, to treat others with disdain." He slipped the noose over the man's head and tightened it around his throat.

"I'm going to disabuse you of that belief. If I had time, I would crucify you. But time is something I'm short on. See, this . . . " He gestured to encompass the Jewish neighborhood around them. "This is personal, this I am doing because I want to. This is a kindness compared to what is coming for Dragan Risti. When your soul leaves your body, dancing at the end of this rope, I want your dybbuk to tell him who did this. I want him to know that his past comes seeking blood and retribution. Let those words scream from your lost soul as it is pulled into your hell." Malechai grabbed the squirming man and tossed him from the roof.

He fell a few feet before the noose, tied to a stair

banister, caught him and broke his neck. He swung, lifeless and mutilated, for all to see.

Malechai stood watching for a moment, then made his way back down the stairs beside the building and moved towards the house he had seen the little girl in. Not bad, not a single shot was fired. But it would still not be long before the priest knew what happened here. Perhaps the man's dybbuk would truly deliver the message; anything was possible. But even if it didn't, when these men failed to show up and they found the corpses Mal had left strewn about, there would be blood to pay. He knocked on the door to the house.

"What do you want?" a shaky voice replied, the accent thick. Mal answered in Yiddish.

"The guards are dead. If you stay here, their friends will come and finish what they started."

The door creaked open, and a young man with a scruffy beard appeared. *"Dead?"* He looked past Mal and saw the gore and mess that Mal had left of the two guards in the main thoroughfare. He looked pale and sick at the sight.

"Dead," Mal agreed. *"And if you don't want you and your daughter to join them, gather up everyone, hide your tallits and your kippah, and make your way west. Get out of town now."*

"That is a dangerous journey."

"Less dangerous than remaining here. Head to San Francisco; there are more Jews there, and less murderous priests." Mal didn't know that for sure, but there was a decent Jewish population that seemed to be doing okay from what he had seen when he had passed through that town.

The man seemed to consider for a moment, his fear of the unknown battling with his fear of the pogrom here at home.

"The priest consorts with Mallikim and seeks our death. I will stop him, but I will not be able to protect our people. I am asking you to do this mitzvah. Preserve lives

and head to San Francisco." Mal repeated the statement wrapped in the language of Torah and duty. That did it.

The man nodded and disappeared back inside, already calling to his family. In his place, the young girl appeared, staring up at Mal.

"Ma'am."

"Thank you."

Mal nodded at the girl's thanks, knowing it would probably be the closest thing he got to gratitude in this cursed place, and turned to leave. He had too much to do, and every minute he procrastinated would be another minute that the priest could prepare for the coming storm.

CHAPTER FIVE

BIG TROUBLE IN LITTLE BRODIE

MALECHAI WALKED DOWN the main street, the mastiff stalking next to him. At the moment, no one but he and the Jewish population of the city knew about the murders. When those became public, when they saw what he had left of the men, then he would need to be a bit less brazen. He didn't know if he would be, at that point. Intimidation was a potent tool, playing on people's fears. But fear was a tangible currency here. He was just one more monster in the town of Brodie. He might not even be the worst monster.

Mal passed under the red gate that marked the entrance to Chinatown and paused when he heard Mishpat growl. Glancing back, he watched the golem prowl just outside the gates. Agrat had said the place was warded against demons, but it looked like even the golem was having problems.

"Stay. Wait for me here," he commanded.

The golem didn't like it and let out a full-throated bark before it padded into the shadows of a nearby building, his burning sapphire eyes glowing in the darkness.

Turning from his angry dog, Mal made his way into the Chinese-controlled neighborhood. The smells were a mouth-watering assault on his senses—something about Chinese spices always made him hungry. He looked over the signs that hung on the doors; they were written in

Chinese and English. After a few minutes, he walked into the apothecary.

Behind the counter, an old woman was yelling at her children, and she was so immersed in scolding them for being children she didn't realize she had a potential customer until his shadow fell across her. She turned with a weary smile and then let out a startled yelp when she saw Malechai's disfigured face standing in front of her. The kids pointed, babbling in their own language about the scary-faced man. The woman quickly regained composure and greeted Malechai in broken English.

"Hello, you need some medicine?" she asked, already grabbing jars of salves and balms from a shelf behind her, no doubt assuming he was there to find something to soothe the constant pain his scars caused him.

"I need information," he corrected, sliding a few coins across the counter.

The woman looked him and then the coins. She said some curse in Chinese before passing her hands over the coins, making them disappear.

"I sell medicine, not gossip. You can go to the salon or tea house if you want gossip," she snapped, though with her back turned to him, he could see she was hunched over and looking over the coins.

He didn't move or respond to her grumbling, waiting in silence while she looked over the coins.

She glanced at him, still standing there. "Haiya, you still here?" She turned and rested her hands on the counter, meeting his eyes with her own ferocious gaze. "What you want?"

"I want to know how y'all keep the demons out and how I can drive em out of Brodie," he answered easily. Malechai wasn't a man to beat around the bush.

She waved dismissively. "Ah, I sell medicine, not magic. You can go talk to Lu Feng Xo."

"And where do I find this . . . Loo?" he asked.

"Lu not Loo. Can't even speak right, need better balm

for your face!" She pushed a small tin towards him. "You paid, take it." He didn't argue; he had known women like her. She reminded him of his own mom, strong and defiant, but with a heart of gold. "You can find Lu at the teahouse; just ask."

He tipped his hat to her and left the little shop, looking over the strange characters on the back of the tin. Who knew what was in it, but he would try it. Hell, couldn't make his face any uglier than it already was. The teahouse was easy to find, a two-story building on a corner. It was obviously the center of Chinatown's social life. It was bustling with activity.

The activity all but stopped as Mal approached. People stared as he passed, unashamedly commenting in whispers to each other about the scarred Jew in their midst. Mal ignored them; he wasn't vain enough to care what people said about his face; hell, he wasn't here looking for company. He strode through the doors, ignoring the silence that descended on the teahouse, and sat down at an empty table. He was the only non-Chinese in the place, and his scarred face was obviously garnering some attention on its own. He figured they must think their protective spells had failed and he was a demon, that or a representative from Brodie here to make life hard for them.

A young Chinese woman approached his table; she looked defiant, as if challenging him to make trouble. "What you want, mister?" she asked.

He made a show of looking over the menu, a pointless act as he couldn't read a goddamned word of their language. "Looking for Lou Feng Sho," Mal finally said, setting down the menu. "Was told I could find him here."

The waitress looked confused and shook her head, wordlessly communicating her lack of comprehension.

"Damnit, Lou, Loo, Lu." He tried to remember how the woman at the medicine shop had said it.

"Lu Feng Xo?" she asked suddenly, looking pleased with herself when he nodded. She walked away and came back a few minutes later with an older man whose beard hung well past his chest. He sat down and muttered something to her. She ran off.

"I assume you're Lu?" Mal asked, then sat in silence as the other man simply glared at him from across the table. They sat like that until the waitress came back and set two cups of tea on the table.

Lu said something in Chinese before lifting his cup and sipping. The waitress played translator. "Master Xo want to know what is it you want with him."

Mal glanced at the waitress, then back at Lu before shrugging; he had used translators before; the world was wide, with more languages than there were people, as far as he could tell.

"You protect your people with magic. My people didn't have that benefit. I want to take the fight to the demons, looking for any help that I can get," Mal explained, getting right to the point.

Lu's eyebrows shot up in surprise as the waitress translated for him. He spoke a string before laughing—was a deep laugh that seemed more bemused than amused.

"Master Xo says that it is strange to hear a Westerner talk so openly of magic and demons. He had thought you were all spineless or blind."

Mal chuckled, lifting his cup and taking a sip. The tea was warm and good but not nearly as satisfying as a shot of vodka would have been. "Yeah, I can see that. But I have eyes, and I see evil rising in Brodie, an evil I aim to put an end to."

The waitress and the old man spoke back and forth for a few moments, arguing, it appeared, while Mal sipped the tea, waiting for one of them to speak in a language he could understand. The argument became more and more heated. Finally, the waitress seemed to give in and dropped her head and hands.

"Master Xo offers you a test to prove you have the skill to do as you say and the compunction to help others." She glared at him from the corner of her eyes. She was angry and scared. "Many of the younger women of our community have been taken. There is a hotel, Lola's Goat, where they are being kept and . . . " She trailed off, not wanting to spill her thoughts on the monstrous nature of the sex trade and its xenophobic cruelty.

"And you want me to put a stop to it. Or he does. Why don't you want that?" Mal asked, leaning forward. He tried to look and sound sincere, but the constant smirk of his scarred face and the guttural accent he spoke with made him sound cruel and callous.

"I want it done by Chinese! Why should we trust a júwàirén to help us when you are the ones who are stealing my sisters? Why should saving my friends be a test and not a priority?" She spat the words at him.

Mal didn't know the word júwàirén, but he understood the sentiment. It was like *goyim*. She didn't want her family and friends' fate resting in the hands of an outsider. But Mal didn't care what she wanted or what she needed. Having Chinese magic and part of the town on his side would make his efforts in Brodie easier, and so he would take their test, free their girls, and add their tally-whackers to his tally for Agrat. He set down his cup of tea and nodded.

"Where is this hotel?" Mal asked.

He had done this kind of work before. People always went after young girls. And other people always wanted their daughters back. Sometimes it was the same people. One constant, those who stole children were weak, shit-fucking cowards.

"To the Northwest of town, close to the mines," she answered, not needing to translate first.

Mal nodded, finished his tea, and stood, making his way towards the door. "I'll be back, either with the girls or with blood money."

The waitress started crying at his words, but he was already gone.

Five dead so far, and more to come, and it wasn't even noon yet. Mal preferred to work in the dark of night, when shadows and men's natural inclination for drink and slumber would make them easier targets. But when Agrat had mentioned that the synagogue had been burned down, he had let the fire in his belly rise up and had acted rashly. Now, he was sitting on a ticking time bomb. As soon as the law knew about the bodies, so would Risti. Mal doubted Risti would know it was him, but he would know someone was acting against him. Once he started striking against the power structure and the priest's safety net, hell was sure to follow.

Mal looked up at the whorehouse that had been converted from a motel—at least, that's what he assumed had been done. A small wooden sign hung above the door, proclaiming it to be Lola's Goat. The building looked like a motel, had all the trappings of a place for miners without a roof over their heads to call it a night. But a red lantern hung above the door, unlit for the moment. The doors hung open, and an old woman was sweeping dust and grit out the door. She looked exhausted but bored. Trafficking unwilling women into a constant stream of rape and suicide just wasn't exciting for her. They weren't white women, so to her, it just didn't matter. Maybe Malechai was being unfair. Maybe this woman was just as much a victim as anyone else. Maybe she had been used up and when people stopped paying for her body, she had been relegated to cleaning up after them. Maybe. Mal walked straight towards the woman.

She finally looked up, scowling at his ugly face. "We're closed for the day; you can come back du . . . " she started to say.

He drew his gun, set the barrel against her cheek, and before she could even utter a plea, blew her jaw off in a spray of blood, bone, and teeth. He reached forward with his other hand, grabbed her tongue as it flopped uselessly in the open wound, and pulled her out of his way. There were shouts and a commotion from inside; it was time to deal with that.

Mal moved into the bar and was met by several men. They were all fumbling with their pistols or diving behind cover as Mal came in. He stayed calm; pistol already drawn as it was, they couldn't hope to draw before he fired. He took his time lining up each shot. The man near the stairs took a bullet in the throat; he gurgled around the blood gushing through the wound as he sunk to his knees. The man who was trying to get behind the bar he shot in the elbow and then the knee, dropping him onto the ground to pull himself through his own blood to try to get behind cover. The last man, the one who had been on the stairs, actually did get his gun out, but his shot was rushed and went wide. Before he could calm his hand, Mal shot him, once in the thigh and once in the upper left chest. His heart burst in a spray of meat and vitae as he tumbled over the railing.

Malechai looked around, listening for more trouble, but only heard the frantic breathing and prayers of the man behind the bar. He popped open the chamber of his revolver and ejected the spent casings, then grabbed a handful of bullets and reloaded as he calmly walked behind the bar to stand over the bleeding, praying man.

"Howdy."

"The fuck you want? Why are you doing this?" the man screeched up at him.

Malechai turned his head. Did this piece of shit really not understand what was happening? Did he not understand that you reap what you sow and he had sown an entire crop of blood and vengeance? Malechai knelt next to him and grabbed his collar, pulling him up. The man shouted in pain as pressure was put on his knee.

"Who oversees taking the girls?" Malechai asked calmly.

"Fuck you!"

"Rude." Malechai raised his gun and held the length of the barrel against the man's ear. He fired.

The man screamed, twisting in Mal's grasp as blood ran from his ruptured eardrum.

Mal pressed the hot metal into the man's chin, forcing him to turn his good ear towards Mal. "Who oversees kidnapping the Chinese girls?" he asked again.

The man blubbered, weakly scrabbling at Mal's arm. "It's Danny. Danny takes charge of all that. Please, I don't got nothing to do with it, I just tend the bar, please."

Mal nodded and pressed the barrel of his gun against the man's other ear and fired five times. The man howled, and as he did, Mal rammed the now empty, super-heated gun down the man's mouth.

He hit the back of the man's throat, triggering his gag reflex and forcing him to throw up. As the vomit came up, it sizzled and popped around the barrel of Mal's gun. The warm liquid sloshed around his hand, but Mal didn't move away. He forced the man's head up, holding him there as he choked to death on his own boiling regurgitate.

Mal dropped the dead man and set his gun on the counter. Seeing a bottle of clear alcohol nearby, he grabbed a rag off the counter, wet it, and wiped off his piece—he would need to do some more maintenance before he went into a firefight, but the trusty hunk of iron had been through worse. There was screaming now from upstairs, and Mal could hear the sounds of people struggling with doors. He sighed heavily and reloaded the pistol before heading up to the second floor. He saw rows of doors along the hallway, each one locked with a padlock from the outside. Keeping the girls prisoners. Hell, probably keeping them locked up with their johns all night.

Mal looked over the padlocked doors for a moment before heading back downstairs and poking through the corpses, looking for the keys. He found them on the bartender. He looked down at the man, whose eyes had bulged almost comically as he had suffocated, and shook his head. He wouldn't close the man's eyes. He wouldn't give him that respect. On top of just being scum, the man had been a liar too. Mal took the keys and proceeded up the stairs. He unlocked the first door to find a young Chinese woman huddled in the corner, trying to hide under the wadded-up sheets of her bed.

"You speak English?" he asked; the woman didn't answer. He went to the next room and opened the door. Another woman stood there; she had taken the gun out of her John's belt and was aiming it at him. Mal looked at her, and then down at the unconscious man. "How about you? You speak English?"

Slowly, fearfully, the woman nodded.

"Good. I'm going to unlock each of these doors. You come behind, get all your people dressed, and then you all run along back home. Understand?" Mal asked.

The woman nodded again.

Good enough for Mal; he raised the gun lazily and shot the passed out drunk in the bed. Ignoring the woman's screams, he turned and moved to continue unlocking doors. Each room held a woman, or a child, in various states of undress. All looked underfed, bruised, and dead on the inside. Some of the rooms had men in them, unconscious or struggling to get dressed. One had even been beating on the door when Mal had opened it. Luckily, Mal had reacted faster, head-butting the man back, kicking him in the balls, and then cutting his throat with his snake knife before the man could even parse what was happening. Finally, Mal opened the last door, the only door on the floor that wasn't locked.

"Don't you move, fuckhole!" Inside was a fully dressed man holding a girl, probably no more than ten years old, in front of him. His gun was pressed to the girl's temple.

Mal looked around the room. No adults other than the man.

"Now you step the fuck back, and you put your hands

up, or this little spit fire here gets to return to her momma in a bucket, you hear me, stranger?"

Mal ignored the man, glancing to the side as the woman he had spoken to earlier helped the others flee. She paused, looking at Mal; she obviously knew who was in the room, she obviously understood the situation. He nodded at her, giving her permission to worry about her own skin and run. As she headed down the stairs, Mal turned his attention to the man who hadn't stopped yelling.

"You're Danny," he offered finally.

"What?" The man asked, caught off guard by the use of his name.

"You're Danny. You are the one who has been stealing the girls."

"What are you, some gun for hire? The Chinese hire you?" He tilted his head, a mean grin spreading across his face. "I'll be damned, Mexicans and Chinese working together against the white man. Just as Father Risti said would come to pass."

Malechai considered correcting him, but the truth was, he wouldn't be alive long enough to get it wrong twice.

Danny continued. "Now you're going to throw down your weapons and back up." Danny gestured with the gun to indicate where Mal should toss his own weapons.

But as soon as the gun was off the girl's head, Mal shot from the hip, shattering Danny's shin with a bullet. The little girl screamed as she was dropped, and she ran for the door. He was empty again. Spending bullets on these scum like they were free. He charged forward, drawing his still bloody knife as he dashed past the girl, and rammed his shoulder into Danny's chest. As they went down, Mal pinned Danny's gun arm with his elbow and slammed the knife into his gut, dragging the blade through clothes, skin, and intestines. Tossing the knife aside, Mal reached into the hole he had cut and began ripping out organs, tearing flesh from its place, and tossing things aside even as Danny struggled under him.

Mal kept tearing, his eyes locked calmly on Danny's as he worked. He stared him down even as he sent the man's soul to Sheol. The man grew weaker and weaker under Mal until, finally, his eyes glossed over in death.

Mal stood. He was covered in blood; he wouldn't be able to just waltz through town anymore. Shrugging, Mal turned and saw that Danny had been keeping clothes here. He was evidently a predator who liked to enjoy his prey at any time. Mal glanced down at the corpse. He didn't want to touch the rapist's tool, but a deal was a deal, and he couldn't afford to be choosy. He knelt down, pulled Danny's pants off, and sawed off his unimpressive dick. He would take a few minutes to go back and harvest all the men he had killed here to add to the bag. And the three downstairs too. Not bad for one stop.

Malechai changed into some of the clothes he found, keeping his tallit and kippah. He pushed the blood-stained tallit underneath the highwayman's duster, hiding the evidence of his murders as he headed down the stairs, ready to grab the last three cocks from their dead owners before returning to Chinatown.

He paused at the top of the stairs, seeing half a dozen men standing around the saloon. The little girl he had just freed was struggling in the arms of a very large man. Perhaps man wasn't the right term for what was holding the girl. His too round eyes glowed the dull red of cooling embers, and he wore a shiny star on his shirt. He looked like a flesh-colored toad, so swollen and bulbous; his mouth was too wide, and his lips were so thin as to almost be nonexistent. Every few moments, a tongue, thick and purple, licked at the thin lips, leaving a trail of mucus-thick slime that he sucked back into his mouth with a noisy slurp. Bony growths dotted his wide head and visible skin— they looked like ossified moles or the tiny barbs you would see on a rosebush. The sickly sweet stench of body odor and dried sweat wafted from the toad-man, overpowering even the coppery smell of the blood Mal had spilled.

Seeing Malechai coming down the stairs, the creature smiled, revealing a mouth with too many teeth. He released the girl, who ran out the door screaming the entire way. Malechai looked around the room. No one was pointing a gun at him. Which meant that they felt no fear. They were trying to intimidate him. Mal continued down the stairs and pulled the knife out as he reached the bottom. That caused several of the men to draw iron and stiffen, but not the demon; he remained calm. Mal knelt and started the grisly work of separating the dead man from his manhood.

"Them for Agrat?" The swollen sheriff finally asked, his voice like gravel being ground to dust with the thick slur of a Cajun accent.

"She make this deal before?" Mal asked in response, standing and pulling the burlap sack from his belt to drop in his trophy, then casting about for the second man who had fallen from the railing. No one else moved as he found the man and got to work.

"She try to, ain't no one ever accept before." The demon—had to be Beliya'al—chuckled, shaking his head, a long mucus covered tongue slipping out of his mouth as he spoke. "You the one that done killed them men over east side."

"Are you arresting me?"

"I do believe what you doin' might be considered illegal," the infernal sheriff said in answer.

Mal stopped and stood, meeting the thing's eyes. His hands hovered near his pistol, but even he wouldn't be able to get off any shots, surrounded as he was by armed men. "Is it? These men were stealing women for rape, not just women but girls." Several of the humans looked sickened, only Beliya'al remained unfazed. "I freed the girls, maybe some casualties in doing so, but call it a citizen's execution of criminal elements. I was helping you."

"And them men that was watching over the Jews, how was that helpin' the law?" the swollen demon asked, almost conversationally.

Malechai turned his head, counting the men. Even if Mishpat were to leap into the inn and join the carnage, he doubted he could get more than a couple of shots off before he was gunned down. "I wouldn't know about those men," he finally answered. A lie, one that everyone knew was bullshit.

The air was thick with tension as each mortal man tallied their chances of making it out alive. The moment was shattered when the bulbous demon began laughing.

"Ah shit, listen here, boy, I'm the law. Me. I make 'em, I uphold 'em, I decide what is and isn't. For all your purposes here in Brodie, I am the alpha and omega. But here's the thing. All this? All this is too easy. Too boring. I'm bored, boy! Let's discover together where this goes. When all said and done, I'll add your dick to that pile there and hand it over to Agrat. Once I finish with her myself." He pushed himself to his feet and nodded, signaling his men to leave.

Mal said nothing to the threat. He was outgunned at the moment, and he would need to be smarter if he was going to have any chance at all of surviving this task. He watched the men file out, and once they were clear, he moved behind the bar to relieve the last corpse of his ill-used burden. Thirteen, just over one tenth of what he needed to collect. A lesser man might have qualms, or at least questioned the blood and sin he was soaking his immortal soul in. But Malechai ben Palache was no lesser man, and he felt no guilt for the Christian blood he spilled on the sands of Brodie.

CHAPTER SIX
FOR YOU HAVE CAST ME INTO THE DEEP

Y THE TIME Malechai made it back to Chinatown, the sun was high in the sky and blazing down on him. Another reason to work at night when the sun was down, but he didn't have too many choices now. The sheriff had started a game of cat and mouse, one that Malechai did not yet have all the pieces in place to play. Mishpat again waited at the gates of Chinatown as Malechai walked through the streets. People stared at him now. He wasn't just some round-eye asshole who was sticking his nose where it didn't belong . . . now he was some round-eye asshole who had brought them back their daughters, sisters, and mothers. Almost all of them looked worried. Scared of the retribution the town would visit on them for the bloodshed Malechai had unleashed.

It was idiotic, is what it was; blood would be spilled no matter what actions Mal took. They could die like cowards giving up their women, or they could die like men with steel in their hearts. Risti wouldn't allow anyone other than white Christians to occupy his city. Mal hoped that these Chinese understood that. Their time was limited unless they dealt with the issue first, or more likely, unless they helped Mal deal with it.

As he walked, a man ran up beside him babbling in Chinese. Mal didn't understand him, but he did understand when the man offered a small package wrapped in paper. A thank you in the form of food. Mal's third favorite form of thanks, after vodka or pussy. Why take money when you could just get the things you would buy with it anyway?

He pushed open the batwing doors to the teahouse and stepped in. It fell deadly silent. Everyone in the restaurant was staring at him. He saw the waitress he had spoken to earlier cradling the little girl who Danny had been threatening. It was good the women had made it back. Mal sat at an empty table and unwrapped the food he had been handed. It was a small bread roll, warm to the touch. He bit into it and was surprised by the meat inside. Damn good, probably not Kosher, but neither was killing a bunch of men and sleeping with a demon. Mal took another bite. Fucking good. A man hastily brought Mal a cup of tea and set it on the table. Mal watched him, but the man said nothing, simply setting it down and retreating. After a few moments, the old man, Lu Feng Xo, joined him and sat at the table with Mal. They sat in silence, Mal eating and Xo sipping tea while they waited for the waitress to step forward to translate once more. When she did, her eyes were puffy and red from crying.

"I did not expect you to return," Xo said finally. "I expected you to die, or more likely, to run and seek your answers somewhere else."

Mal shook his head. "I told you I would be back with the girls or blood money. Hope you preferred to have your women alive. Hope you also plan to uphold your end of our little agreement." He met the old sorcerer's eyes, his own narrowed in warning. Xo didn't seem afraid.

"What exactly do you want, júwàirén? If it is within the powers of our community, it will be yours. You wish to ward your home or community from the demons?" Xo said, leaning back and producing a long-stemmed pipe, which he lit and puffed on while waiting for Mal to make his demands.

Mal set the now empty fabric his lunch had been in on

the table, washing down his last bite with a gulp of tea. As soon as he set the cup down, a waiter rushed forward to fill it. Mal watched the man retreat again. "Already protected my community, don't got a home here. No, I need something to kill demons."

The waitress paused, looking at Mal wide-eyed before she repeated the words in Chinese.

Xo laughed at that, but when he saw Mal was not laughing, he stopped. He spoke quietly, quickly, and when he was finished, he summoned over a man and spoke to him while the waitress translated.

"Master Xo says that while what you ask is not impossible, it is not so simple as warding a place against their kind. What we need will take many parts, parts that are not cheap nor easy to come by, especially in America." Xo turned his attention back to Mal as a large, locked chest was brought out from the back and placed on the table before him. As he spoke, she translated. "First, you must make them unstable, bring about emotional distress; this will loosen their hold on our world. Next, you must deal grievous harm to their physical forms."

"That part at least won't be an issue," Mal noted.

Xo nodded, as though Mal's propensity for harm was obvious, which if the women from the brothel had spoken, maybe it was.

"Lastly, you must attach a charm, and perform some action that will sever their connection entirely, this will send them back to hell." Xo unlocked the chest and pulled out several items. Stacks of rectangular fabric, an inkwell, and a long brush. Finally, he pulled out a curved ram's horn.

"A shofar!" Mal exclaimed, surprised.

The waitress shook her head. "It is the horn of a goat. If you blow . . . " She paused as Mal reached across the table.

"I know how to blow a damn shofar, woman." He turned the horn over in his hands; it wasn't that surprising that exorcism rituals held common actions. Different beliefs, sure, but all the same world. He brought the horn to his lips and let out a t'ruah, the stuttering breath of a staccato blast, before taking a deep breath and blasting out a tekiah gedolah. The note, clear and low, hung in the air as he blew the shofar. All eyes in the tea house turned to him, and the conversation died out. He hadn't blown the Shofar since he was a kid, but it felt good, it felt natural.

Xo nodded. "It is good you know how to blow the horn. It dissipates negative chi, and the demons will be unable to remain in our realm." He handed his pipe off to the man who had brought the box. "Come back tonight and I will have charms ready for you." He paused, sitting back as Malechai looped a bit of rawhide around the horn to secure it to his belt. "Understand, none of this will protect you from them. You can choose to defend yourself or you can choose a path of violence. You walk towards death, arms outstretched, bathing in the blood. But those who walk in blood answer in it as well."

Malechai nodded. "I know that. I'll wait here, if it's all the same to you." Malechai sat back and pushed his hat back away from his eyes as he leaned back. While he was sure he would be more comfortable waiting in Agrat's bed, he was also sure the succubus wouldn't let him sleep. He needed to be rested, and what safer place was there than Chinatown, where the demons couldn't trespass? He rose, aiming to leave Xo alone to do his work, when he spotted a table covered in tiles. He waved over the waitress.

"What's that?" he asked, pointing.

"Oh, that's just a game called Mahjong," she stuttered.

Malechai watched them play for a moment, watched the money exchange hands. No one was playing cards, which he would have preferred, but since he was going to be here a while waiting on the old sorcerer to make his charms, he might as well learn a new skill and lose some money. "Teach me," he ordered her, grabbing a nearby chair and dragging it to the table, much to the chagrin of the men already playing. When Mal produced a stack of silver coins, the complaints simmered down. Greed was always a good grease towards friendship, even through a language barrier.

Hours later, Mal grumbled as he slid his last couple of coins across the table. It was a complex game, one of chance and strategy. It reminded him of the card game Rummy, which he had learned from Spanish soldiers back in the old world. He liked this one more. The tiles felt good to slide around the table. The complexity and the art spoke of intention. Something Mal could get behind. He just wished he had done better. Now he would have to rifle through the pockets of corpses to restock his funds.

He slid his chair out, offering the men who were a bit richer now a short respectful bow as he had seen other Chinamen do, and moved to where Xo was sitting. The old man was massaging his hands, which, judging from the number of little fabric pieces he had written on, had cramped up something terrible. The Sorcerer looked up at Mal and smiled wryly.

When Xo spoke, it was with exhaustion scratching at his throat. "Once you have inflicted your rage on the Móguǐ, place a charm on their body and blow the horn. This is all we can do for you."

Malechai picked up the stack of fabric rectangles and looked over them. These were the charms, he assumed. He pushed them into his pocket, nodding his thanks, then he turned and left without another word.

Just outside the door, the waitress stopped him. "Wait, please . . . thank you. I just wanted to thank you." She stared up at the scarred, terrifying murderer. "And to give you this." She offered him a silver disk, a medallion of some sort. Printed on it was a figure of a robed Chinese warrior wielding a huge guandao, a guandao only outsized by the warrior's flowing beard. "This is Guan Yu, the god of war. If you walk into battle, there is no need to walk alone."

Mal looked at the coin, rolling it between his knuckles. He didn't put any faith in gods other than his own, but he wouldn't turn down the gift. Hell, could be worth a pretty penny. He slipped it in his shirt pocket and nodded before turning and leaving Chinatown.

It was night already. Malechai made his way back west, following the same path he had walked when he had gone to get the girls. He passed plenty of miners, but as he approached the saloon, there was a lot of panic, people calling for someone to go get the sheriff, calling for someone to call the doctor. Doctor wouldn't do them any good. Mal had checked the corpses of the men before harvesting them. Mal was tempted to make a stop at the brothel. Anyone stopping there now was stopping there because they were hoping to partake in stolen flesh. And his fingers itched to put more men in the ground. But he kept his head down as he passed the miners, ignoring the commotion. His business there was done.

Back during the January Uprising when the Palache siblings had first cut their teeth in war, a fellow Pole had accused Malechai and his sister of being nothing but bloodthirsty killers, that they had taken the acts of violent brutality too far in dealing with the enemy. Malechai had assured him, and then his commanders, that he only did his gory work to see the day won. But if that had been true, wouldn't he have sought peace in the aftermath? Instead, he and his siblings had taken their bloody skills to the market, selling his sword and his gun to the highest bidder. He had seen the Schleswig War, fought against the Bukhara in the conquest of Tashkent. He had fought under the Spanish flag, the British flag, for the Dutch, the Russians, the Austrians, and the Germans. A never-ending slog through the corpses of enemies who weren't even his enemies. He had seen the true nature of man, and to fear demons was foolish when compared to the evil that plain human scum were capable of. Himself included. But Malechai felt no remorse for the evil he had done. He had put more men in the ground than was his fair share, and the thought of killing a hundred more didn't hurt his heart none. It made his heart race. It prickled his flesh and in turn quickened his step.

Americans spoke of their terrible civil war, but he saw no evidence of the war-torn nation they had described to him on the boat. No, this country seemed whole, it seemed held together, unlike the ruins of ancient cities that lay scattered like so much dust and dreams across the European countryside. Perhaps that was the benefit of being new, of being built of wood, spit, and blood instead of stone. Rebuilding was easier when it was a poor excuse for a building in the first place. The heat and the scorpions and spiders that stalked every step in this cursed land brought a foreboding darkness to the American landscape. But Malechai was damned and determined that he should be the most terrifying thing to stalk the streets of Brodie, damn these demons back to the box if they stood between him and Risti.

His trip to the mines would serve several purposes. According to Agrat, a demon named Baladan ran the mines. He would need to kill that demon, or at least convince it to break its own ward. Most of the miners were heading home for the day, but Mal was guessing there would be guards, miners who were desperate to make coin and so stayed late, and he doubted the demons ever slept. Maybe they did. Agrat had at least pretended to sleep. But Mal was banking on the mines at night being the best time to do some real damage to the town without murdering every single citizen of Brodie.

When he reached the mines, he set down the burlap sack and stood for a few moments, looking at all the entrances. Little holes for little ants to dig into and attempt to find a better life for themselves. Each one could be collapsed. And that had a certain appeal to it—collapse the entrances, trap them all inside with a dwindling supply of air and little to no food but collapsing all the tunnels leading into the dark depths of the earth would probably take all night, and likely, as soon as he collapsed one, the others would flee. And to top it all off, there was no guarantee that the demon, Baladan, would even be put out by a lack of oxygen.

The other option he thought of was just going down into the mines to kill whoever he ran into, but that, too, would be more trouble than it was worth—he could get lost, could be ambushed There really wasn't a great solution to his current predicament. He moved through the area, considering each mine entrance, trying to discern if there was something he could see, some piece to the puzzle that could help him discern how he could crack this nut, how he could determine which mine entrance led him to his quarry. He glanced down at the massive mastiff next to him and sighed.

"Don't suppose you can sniff him out?" he asked the golem.

It looked at him, tilting its head in confusion before letting out a low whining growl, as if in question. It may look like a hound, but it wasn't an actual dog; it was an inert piece of mud given sentience and malice by a beleaguered and broken people in need of a savior.

Mal almost chuckled at that thought—any person or group that pinned their hopes on him and a dog-shaped pile of mud were more than desperate; they were already lost.

He walked the entire length of the quarry, but no entrance gave any more information than any other. Hundreds of little holes dotting the side of the man-made cliffs filled with the guilty, the innocent, and riches. Malechai paused and leaned against the stones of the dam that kept the river at bay, resting his legs while considering his options. These mines were why Brodie had grown, what had attracted the priest in the first place. Other sins might damn a man, but greed damned everyone around them. Now the greed of those who had stayed late would be paid for with interest. Malechai went back down to the storehouse near the mine's entrance, wasting no time breaking the padlock keeping the simple shack closed, and rummaged inside for a bit, finding everything he needed. He also grabbed a discarded pair of saddlebags. He tied off the burlap sack and tossed the whole mess with the scavenged supplies and his gifts for Agrat onto Mishpat's back. The hound looked at him quizzically but accepted the burden. Then the two of them trudged back across to the far side of the mines.

The back and forth he was doing across the mines and Brodie reminded him of being a kid and scanning the lines of Torah with his grandfather, back when Zeyde had been alive. His grandfather had been a hard man, pious but dangerous. He had taught Malechai that the most important rule of all was preserving your own life and that any mitzvot broken in the pursuit of that shouldn't be counted. He hadn't put up with any bullshit and was as quick to slap one of the siblings for flapping their lips during prayers as he was to hug them tight. When Malechai was seven, his Zeyde had taught him to shoot, much to his mother's horror. *He may not be a man yet, but that does not mean he should not know how to be a man!* Mal smiled at the memory as he set pushing the sticks of dynamite into the dam and using the spool of fuse wire to connect them all.

So far, he had killed men guarding houses and a tavern full of rapists. So far, he had been mostly ignored by the powers that be. That ended now. He lit the fuse he had made and took several large steps away from the edge of the quarry. He quickly ducked behind a large stone and took several long breaths, whispering in Yiddish under his breath.

"Blessed one, creator of all, behold the flood I bring to mine enemies. There will be no rainbow at the end of these rains; I will punctuate the sin you allow to run amok in

gun smoke and screams. Brodie is a Sodom, a Gomorrah. Where the rules of decency go unheeded. And, Lord, if you don't plan to do nothing about it . . . " The explosion shook the world; immediately, the rage of the river was let loose, and it filled the quarry in astonishing speed. *"Then I will."*

Malechai finished, rising from behind his shelter. The water was a mass of rapids. White water crashing across every nook and cranny, furious torrents flowing into the mines and filling the mountain with water. How many men, he wondered, how many men died in the first minute? He walked to the edge of the quarry, now the shore of an unleashed river, and watched as the bodies began to rise to the surface of the water. They were battered and broken, the sweep of the water rushing into the tunnels crushing them against the walls of the mines before carrying them out into the more open water. Mal wished he had a cigar to enjoy while watching the dead. His fingers brushed the handle of the knife tucked into his belt. It would take a while to harvest Agrat's bounty but should be worth the effort.

He noticed not all the forms escaping the mine tunnels were dead, and not all of them were human.

Curious, Mal watched one of the figures claw its way through the water and onto the shore. It wore clothes like all the other miners, but its face was stretched out and canine, like a wolf or mongrel. Fur covered its visible skin, and its eyes were tiny sunken things that reminded Mal of swine. He reached into his coat and took one of the charms out as he approached the figure, which lay panting on the shore. Idly, he wondered if Agrat would accept demonic cocks as part of her payment.

When he reached the creature, he delivered a rib shattering kick to its side, forcing it onto its back, and planted his boot on its neck. "Howdy." he said as he put pressure on its throat. "Tell me, you Baladan?"

The thing snapped its jaws at Mal, snarling through yellowed and jagged teeth. All show.

Malechai put his full weight down, crushing its windpipe. He didn't use the charm yet, instead he reached down and grabbed the creature's leg and started dragging it as it struggled towards the next demonic figure sputtering on the shore.

Reaching the figure, he pulled out his gun and fired off four shots, blowing out the creature's elbows and knees. He dropped the struggling demon he had been dragging to the ground and, without responding to the howls of pain and rage from the wounded demon, pulled out his knife and began carving pieces off the first demon. He glanced up as he pulled the demon's pants down, delivering a cruel punch whenever it flailed too much.

"What do you know," he finally said, addressing the demon he had shot, "you do have peckers." He began cutting it off with big sloppy cuts. It watched him work on his fellow with widening, horrified eyes. When Mal dropped the demonic phallus into his bag, shoved a charm into the gaping hole of the demon's crotch, the thing finally stopped struggling. "Now." He met the yellow jaundiced eyes of the demon. "Where is Baladan?"

And so it went, Malechai walking the angry shore of the quarry river, dealing death, banishment, and castration as he went. It was dirty work, but Malechai didn't mind the blood and screams as he sliced through the thin skin and flaccid meat. Each body he passed contributed to his burden. He worked efficiently until he came upon a demon that was alert and standing, as though waiting for Mal to reach him.

Though dressed, this demon was barefoot, and his feet looked like black leathery hands with a thumb on each side of the foot. In the left foot's knuckles, he rolled a silver dollar. He stood almost twice as tall as Malechai but looked to weigh about half as much. A stretched-out characterization of a man mixed with a wolf or mutt is what he looked like to Mal. The figure brushed its sopping wet overalls off with one hand—only four fingers on the actual hands, Mal noted—and stared out of his yellow piggy eyes at the gunslinger.

"What do you hope to accomplish?" Its voice sounded like an entire pack of wild dogs nipping and growling at one another. Somehow, the cacophony of sounds oozed together into pitches that formed the words. It scratched at the insides of Mal's eyeballs to listen to the thing speak.

"Well, I was looking for you," he said slowly, his hand hovering over his gun. He had been reloading as he went but hadn't been keeping a close count on his shots, seeing as there wasn't much excitement and this big boy—Baladan, he was sure—was the first person he saw standing upright. "I figured it was the fastest way to get your attention."

The demon's eyes strayed to Malechai's gun, the lipless muzzle somehow conveying amusement before it tilted its head, spotting the shofar. The amusement fell away. "That was you too then, blowing notes across the mines, sending my sons and daughters to the darkness and shadows of the desert?"

Malechai nodded but didn't speak; he was concentrating on the beastly creature. It seemed rather sure of itself, even after it had watched Malechai kill, dismember, and banish its lesser fellows. Perhaps the demonic mutt-man thought it could kill him before he could do enough damage to banish it.

Baladan tapped his chin with one of his long, triple-jointed fingers. "We've been enjoying this town; we eat the occasional miner who gets lost or injured, we grow our power, but I suppose that is over now. You've destroyed the mines and, in so doing, destroyed Brodie." He stepped forward, ignoring Malechai as he looked over the damage. "I suppose we could rebuild; once you're dead, we could rebuild all of this. Humans will starve and die while we work, but that is a little thing to me. How much pain do you carry, killing so many men to just get to me?" He turned away from the river and looked at Malechai.

Malechai was very aware how much closer the demon was now, how it could get to him in just a couple of steps of his freakishly long legs. Malechai shook his head. "The sad thing is you aren't even the end goal." Mal smiled as he saw the confusion written across Baladan's face. He stepped forward, ducking as he moved and aimed a boot at the creature's ankle. There was a loud crack and down he went.

Malechai wasted no time climbing on top of the flailing demon and wrapping his hands around the thing's scrawny throat. Mishpat leapt forward, biting down on the demon's other leg and shaking his head violently, cracking bone and tearing demonic flesh as he pulled wildly. Baladan roared in pain and rage. His hands wrapped around the mortal man, trying to peel him off, but Malechai was stuck on him like a deer tick in the flesh of a cow. Mal pushed his thumbs into the demon's throat, bearing down with murder in his heart. He couldn't puncture the thing's tough hide, but as he strangled the creature, its flailing got weaker. Mal reached into his pocket for a charm, the neck thin enough to encircle and crush with one hand.

Mal let out a wordless growl as he grabbed one of the scraps of charmed fabric, balled it into a wad, and shoved it into the demon's eye socket. He used his index finger to jam the fabric through, soaking it in blood and vitreous humor. He continued to shove until his knuckles were bumping against the skull of the disgusting creature. Malechai leaned forward, whispering harsh lines of war and condemnation from Torah, then pulled his hand out of the creature's head and grabbed the shofar. He brought it to his lips, ignoring the foul gore coating his hand, and blew a single scathing note into the face of the weakened creature.

Baladan bucked, kicking Mal off him, and breathed deep to let out a screaming, mournful howl of pain. He tried to rise, but his body was smoking and seemed to be melting as he moved. His skin fizzled and popped as it ran down his bones in disgusting rivulets of rancid boiling goo. Within moments, only the blood and sludge-soaked clothing remained of the demon Baladan.

Mal looked down, panting, wondering if he should have cut the cock off before exorcising the creature. Mishpat gagged, making a horrendous sound before he dry heaved once and then vomited up the still bubbling goo that had been Baladan's foot. *You live and you learn*, Mal thought. *Well, some of us live.*

He said a quick, quiet Kaddish for Yitzak before stumbling away from the body of the demon. While on the creature, Mal had been like a golem himself. A statue of unyielding, hateful stone that would not be moved and could not be stopped. But he wasn't a golem of invincible stone. He was a man, and that demon, though gangly, had been strong. He could feel his body protesting as he moved, covered in bruises and welts. He was tired, and when not fueled by rage and violence, his body needed to rest. He considered heading back into town; he could shack back up with Agrat. But again, she wouldn't let him rest, she would expect some action herself.

Malechai chuckled, he wasn't opposed to that sort of night, but there were other considerations too. He reached down and scratched the golem behind the ears, his fingers moving across the strange flesh and fur of the created beast while he thought. He walked up the trail that led out of the mines. He had seen a horse, probably belonging to one of the miners, hitched near the entrance to the mine. He transferred the saddlebags to the horse, relieving his hound, and mounted up.

Truth be told, now that he had broken two of the seals, Risti would be getting feisty. The fear of his defenses and power crumbling around him would be a tangible tension in the air slipping around his neck like a noose. All that meant is that the priest would be hunting for Malechai in force now, and since that toad-thing Baliya'al had confronted him in the whorehouse, everyone would now know his face—even if the thing had let him go after, in the interest of making things "less boring".

Malechai smirked as he overlooked the town of Brodie, his dark eyes focusing on the gathering of torches as a posse was being formed to investigate the explosions. "Am I making it interesting for you yet, demon?" He turned the horse and rode, but instead of heading west into town, he headed east out into the wilderness. Hopefully, in the direction of possible allies.

CHAPTER SEVEN
GHOST DANCE

MALECHAI WAS NOT the tracker his sister was; she would already be on the path to finding what he was looking for. He sat on the horse on the largest hill he could find and looked over the valley around him. The heat, even in the night, was oppressive. To his back, the lights of Brodie burned. They would be out for blood. He had left a trail of mutilated corpses in his wake, gathering his gruesome trophies from the dead and dying. Malechai glanced over his shoulder; they would be sending out posses for sure, hunting for him. But they had only themselves to blame. They had cast their lots with demons, given over their town to the genocidal maniac Dragan Risti. When one lies down with demonic dogs, it is best to expect to wake up with your dick cut off and a knife through your eye. Malechai turned back towards the valley.

Somewhere down there would be the Paiute, the natives of this land, those who lived here before the colonizers had made it their home. He had heard stories. Savages who cannibalized white men. Practitioners of dark magics and worshipers of evil gods. But Mal had heard these stories before, he had been accused of all these things himself. Every Jew living had. His gun felt heavy in his belt. The urge to turn back and ride into town and die while spilling Christian blood was powerful, but Mal was nothing if not a realist.

With allies, with help, he could spill much more blood than on his own.

Malechai gently kicked his horse, spurring it forward into the valley. He saw no fires burning, but somewhere out there in the darkness, the Paiute waited. Mal rode into the night, though he had been mindful of his tracks as he left the mines, now he simply rode, not trying to hide his presence. After almost two hours of riding, he paused. He could feel eyes on him. He was in a small valley between hills; trees and shrubs dominated the landscape around him, and he realized with some frustration that he had ridden into the perfect spot for an ambush. He slowly raised his hands, leaving the gun and sword at his side. Could he draw and shoot before he was killed by an ambusher? Maybe, but he hoped he would not have to find out. After several minutes of silence, there was a low whistle from the brush.

They emerged from all around him, men with dark reddish skin and untrusting eyes. They wore leather pants and muslin shirts, a motley outfit that seemed made and dyed for the individual rather than in a textile shop like he had been seeing in town. They aimed rifles and bows at him. Mal kept his hands up, wondering if he had miscalculated. But he knew their look—the look of a people displaced, who were dealing with Christian oppressors who demanded conversion and took all you had whether or not you did as they said. Agrat had said they were possible allies, but that would only happen if they didn't kill him out of hand, and if he found someone who spoke English.

"What do you want so far from town?" a voice called. It was deep and resonate, it had the conviction of knowing right from wrong and knowing that wrong was sometimes necessary.

"Looking for Paiute," Malechai responded, narrowing his eyes to peer at the men in the moonlight. It was his first real glimpse of the natives of this land. They did not look kind, but he was a transgressor, an invader in their home.

He was also the lone lamb that was separated from the flock, in danger of incurring the wrath of a people pushed too far. "Was told that we could help one another."

"Help? We are very familiar with the white man's help."

Malechai tipped his hat up, letting the moonlight fall on his ruddy skin. "I'm not one of them. I'm no more welcome in their towns than y'all. I'm here to kill the demons they brought with them."

That set the Paiute to murmuring to each other, seemed most of them spoke English. That was good; he wouldn't have to rely on an emotional waitress to help him communicate. They murmured, but they didn't lower their rifles. It would be a shame to have come all this way only be shot down like a dog before he could finish. Beside him, Mishpat let out a mournful howl, and several of the natives turned their rifles onto the beast, maybe for the first time realizing it wasn't actually a dog.

"You say you are here to fight evil spirits, but you come riding alongside one, stinking of death and blood." One of the Paiute stepped forward. He was older than the others and carried himself with the air of leadership. It was his voice that rang so clearly into the night.

"Mishpat here? Mishpat ain't evil, he's made of earth and mud and made to track and fight evil; there's a difference. As for the blood and death, I told you why I'd come. Did you think I hadn't started yet?" Mal slowly lowered his arms, tired of holding them up. He rested them on the horn of the saddle, watching the natives, waiting for them to either shoot or calm the hell down.

The old man walked forward. His eyes locked on the constructed canine. He held out a hand, muttering under his breath. Malechai frowned; he could feel the subtle pull of energies around the elder. He had seen plenty of strange things in his life, from awful powers unleashed on battlefields and shaman from the north to man-shaped creatures that fed on the corpses that littered the battlefields. He had made deals with a sorcerer, traveled with a golem, and buried his seed deep in the welcoming body of a succubus. But the casual ease with which this native elder seemed to call up power was unnerving. Mal's finger twitched, itching to draw steel. But he sat still, careful and calm.

After a moment, Mishpat rose from his haunches and padded to the elder, rubbing his head against the man's leg affectionately. Mal's frown deepened.

The Elder took a deep breath, reaching down to stroke Mishpat's massive head. "Your beast is a gift from the spirits, a protector, a hunter; he vouches for your purpose. What is your name, Winnemucca?"

"Malechai," he answered simply, looking for at the two of them from his horse. "Don't suppose you could ask your men to lower their guns? Making me a bit nervous having them all on me."

The shaman raised his hand, and the men surrounding Mal melted back into the shadows of the landscape around them, though not a one took their aim off him. He had the impression they were still there, still aiming; he just couldn't see them now. Not exactly comforting.

"I am Pahninee. You have found the A'waggu Dükadü." He turned and began walking away, Mishpat at his heels. Mal rolled his eyes but followed after, assuming that no one directly threatening his life currently was about as warm a welcome as he could expect.

Mal followed Pahninee across the valley and over hills, wondering how far from the town of Brodie this was taking him. He was about to give up and call Mishpat to his side when they topped another hill and the settlement of the Paiute stretched out before him. The houses looked makeshift, tents and homes and small communal buildings that reminded Malechai of yurts. He nodded slightly to himself. He recognized this sort of settlement. It was the sort a nomadic people created when they were forced to settle in one place.

He sat in the saddle there, looking over the village before turning to Pahninee. "I assume you brought me out here for a reason, hopefully to talk on how we can drive the evil out of Brodie."

The elder looked up at him and shook his head. "Brodie itself is evil. If you wish to help the Paiute, if you wish to assist the A'waggu Dükadü, the town itself must be destroyed."

Mal smiled a little at that. Everywhere he went, everyone he met wanted him to up the violence, up the bloodshed; it was the only thing he was really good at. But he shook his head. "I can't kill a town, but I can take care of some of the evil that has descended on it."

Pahninee sighed and shook his head, leading them down into the valley village of the Paiute. At the edge of the settlement, Mal got off the stolen horse and let it graze, trusting whoever had owned it before him had trained it good enough not to run off. He followed the elder as he led Mal to one of the large communal tents.

Inside, a large group had gathered. Men and women were sitting around a small fire, speaking and laughing, but all that stopped as Mal stooped to enter. They glared at him. Several gasped when Mishpat entered next but were calmed by Pahninee as he entered.

"As I said, Winnamucca, you have found us. I am the puhagim of the A'waggu Dükadü. Sit, you are my guest tonight." He strode to the fire and spoke to the others, who sniggered but nodded acceptance of his words.

Malechai glanced at Mishpat, who seemed perfectly content, before sinking down next to the fire. As he sat, someone passed him a bowl of clear broth with chunks of vegetables and white meat floating in it. Briefly, he remembered the rumors of cannibals, but he was suddenly keenly aware of his hunger, and it wouldn't be the first time he had eaten without knowing the source, so he tipped the bowl, slurping. It was chicken. He nodded happily and looked around. Everyone was still staring at him.

"It is customary to share stories when there is a guest," the old man, who was obviously their leader, said to Mal.

Malechai nodded and waited for them to begin, but as everyone continued staring at him, he sighed and stood back up.

"I came here to talk about killing off evil spirits, not tell stories."

"If you wish to deal with our tribe, you must accept our customs while here. If you wish to share our food, you must tell a story. If you wish to sleep here, you must tell a story. If you wish to gain us as allies, you—"

"Must tell a story, I think I get it," Mal grumbled before taking another long slurp from the bowl of soup—it was damn good. "All right, I think I got one for you. My people are from a land similar to this, mountains and desert, sand and stone. It was such a shithole we named it the Land of struggles, Israel. In this time, there were invaders, people from another land; they were pale skinned compared to us, and they made rules. Rules that went against who and what we were as Jews. They tore at our sacred places and kept them for themselves." Malechai paused, seeing a wooden pipe making the rounds. He waited until it got to him—he wasn't a habitual smoker but could use the calm of the tobacco leaf for this story. Taking a few small puffs, he handed the pipe to Pahninee and continued telling the story of the Maccabean revolt the way his granddaddy had told it to him.

"Now these pale fucks, the Greek, they had their own gods, and they sure as hell hated our God. They were afraid of him, and so they tried to destroy him. They thought that God was in a physical place, right? They always think that it's the church or temple that matters, like having a statue of your god is what gives the god power. Seems a bit weak to me. Anyway, they had armies, massive armies they used to conquer and control everything in our land. They kept us from praying, they kept us from eating, they kept us from fucking. They assumed if they took our ability to worship our god the way we wanted to, it would kill our god, it would kill our spirit."

Malechai looked around the assembled Paiute. They hung on his words. Not because of his ability to tell a story, but because they *knew* this story. They had lived this story.

"There was a city on a hill. And a great hero named Yudah, the Lion of the desert . . . " He paused, seeing confusion; they didn't know what a lion was. "The great wolf of Israel decided to make a stand. He had shitty weapons, he had fewer men, he had no supplies. All he had was the elevation, his strength, and the full might of Jewish rage. The Greek army came, and Yudah battered them back. Time and time again his small band fought in the streets, gathering support, and built an army that matched the Greeks, but we fought for our homes, our way of life, while the Greeks fought only for themselves. We slaughtered them. We marched through the mountains, and everywhere a Greek fell, a tree would grow, offering shade and fruit to the Jews. Gratitude from the very land of Israel as we butchered the invaders. To this day, you can walk the valleys of Judea from Hebron to Jerusalem and find the bones of those that think they can destroy the Jews. Find them lying in the shade of the trees that bear the sweetest fruit."

Malechai fell silent then, his eyes thinking back on his grandfather, whose stories of war and bloodshed had always been his favorite.

After several moments, Pahninee cleared his throat. "It is true the white man ignores the puha of the world around them. They designate places to be holy while ignoring the heartbeat of the world around them. Many years before the white man came to these lands, there was a great flood, a flood that swallowed the land."

"I'm familiar." Malechai chuckled. "It was to swallow the wickedness, to cure humanity of the cancer of evil spirits."

The old man nodded in agreement. "But all suffered in the flood, good and bad. The Sagehen survived, found the people. Its heart hurt, our puha called out in anguish to it. And so moved, it built a fire in the sky, a great fire that began drying up the flood waters. The Sagehen believed that she had rescued humankind, but it had dried the flood waters before all evil could be destroyed. Soon, evil found man again. Nŭmŭzóho the cannibal found the people who Sagehen had saved and set upon them.

"His hunger was insatiable, his teeth were made of stone from the mountains, his nails were iron, and his eyes were great fires that found the people wherever they hid. He took the strength of those he ate and turned it upon others, his great hunger never being filled. He stalked the world, seeking to sate a need that was not natural. His teeth cracked bones, and he slurped the marrow of men. His fingernails tore apart women so he could drink their blood. And he delighted the most in the flesh of the children. And so, he exterminated all those Sagehen had saved. His puha overflowed, becoming an unnatural thing too powerful, and it was then that the great wolf intervened. He took the last woman and brought her to the mountains. He taught her the ghost dance, with which she could hide from the flaming eyes of Nŭmŭzóho. He taught her how to weave magic into cloth, to protect her from the teeth of Nŭmŭzóho. And he loved her. After many months, the woman bore four children, two boys and two girls. Two of them were good; these became the Paiute, but two had been infested with the evil of Nŭmŭzóho. To separate them and cease them from fighting, the great wolf set them in the two separate rivers, allowing the waters to decide where to take them."

The elder sighed and shook his head. "But Nŭmŭzóho still hunted the people, and so for many years, the Paiute continued to roam, never staying in one place too long, always practicing the ghost dance to hide from his hungry gaze and weaving our clothes with magic to protect us should he find us."

The assembly fell into silence again as Malechai digested this. It sounded familiar to him. The Flood, the giant cannibals with fire for eyes. It was all legends he had listened to rabbis spew for long decades. But these people, these people so far away, had the same legends. What did that mean? Were they secretly Jews? Jews who had fled from the destruction of their people centuries ago? Were the legends real? Or was there a true universal evil that had struck all people of all lands? Malechai couldn't say. His thoughts were broken as Pahninee spoke again.

"Now we are within Nűműzóho's sight once more. He hides in the garrison of the white men. He cooks their food, feeding them from those he captures. He makes cannibals of them all. This is the evil you seek to face. One who has walked the earth from before time. From before the flood. You will fail, and you will be devoured by the ancient monster."

"Maybe," Malechai finally said. "Probably not. I've already killed one of the demons." He patted the shofar at his side. "I aim to kill at least a few more before all is said and done." Agrat had called the demon at the garrison Tanin'iver, but the Paiute were saying it was this Nűműzóho from their own legends. No wonder the true names of spirits were so hard to find; every damn culture gave the creatures their own little spin on it. Maybe it was their Nűműzóho, or maybe they had forced the reality of a Jewish demon into their own mythology to explain the atrocities they were seeing. Either way, he had a job to do.

"This ghost dance and the magic clothes, what are they?"

"The ghost dance is a sacred ritual, a dance filled with prayer and power that brings our puha into alignment with the natural world. It allows for peace to bloom and also hides us from the sight of evil spirits. It may also be used to unweave the energy of the spirits, undoing the negative harm on the world."

That word *puha* kept coming up. Malechai didn't care enough about the religious beliefs of the Paiute to delve into it, and it sounded like this ghost dance was too much of an intricate thing to be useful in sneaking through town.

"And the clothes?" he asked. "Any chance I can buy some of these magic clothes off you?"

There was laughter in the tent.

"You have nothing we need, Winnemucca, nothing at all. I will not risk my people on the words of a stranger." Pahninee shook his head and rose. "You may sleep in our village tonight. In the morning, go back to Brodie, fight your pointless fight, die your pointless death. But do not return here. You say you have killed one, if it is true, if you can weaken the evil of Brodie enough, we will bring your strength for your battle with Nűműzóho, but do not try to drag us into your death with you."

Malechai nodded and rose as well. It was a fair enough response and one he had been given in the past. Whenever the Jews had looked for allies against the oppression and violence, always there was the underlying hopelessness of trying to fight those in power. He had dealt with two of the demons so far. Agrat and Baladan, that left the banker, the sheriff, and the chef at the barracks that these Paiute feared. A young man gestured for Malechai to follow, but before he did, he turned back to Pahninee.

"Y'all have any knowledge of when the bank's wagons come to town?" he asked.

Pahninee raised an eyebrow but nodded. "We can give you this information in the morning, Winnamucca, in the morning."

"You keep calling me that. What does it mean?"

Pahninee studied Malechai's scarred visage a moment before breaking out in a wide grin. "It means bad-face."

CHAPTER EIGHT

HIS HOUSE OF SILVER AND GOLD

IN THE MORNING, Malechai stepped out of the tent he had been loaned for the night. He had slept in more comfortable lodgings; he had slept in less comfortable places too. He had left his teffilim back in his travel bag at Agrat's place, but he wrapped his blood spotted tallit around his shoulders and over his head and swayed in the cool early morning breeze as he said his morning prayers.

This place was nice; the land wasn't blisteringly cold as it was back home. A young man, hardly more than a boy, walked towards him. The same one who had shown him to the tent? A different man? Malechai couldn't tell. The man wore leather pants and a white rough spun shirt. He carried a bow instead of a rifle, a downgrade from what was available, in Mal's estimation, but he wasn't about to comment on his hosts' choices.

The man stopped and waited for Mal to finish his prayers, his calm brown eyes the color of freshly turned earth staring off at the sunrise. Mal appreciated the quiet moments. The times when the earth seemed to pause, allowing for the barest hints of peace. He imagined it was the feeling that was supposed to happen during Shabbos. It was the feeling that all the Chasidim, hell all the Jews, looked for every week. But Mal only found it in the minutes between waking and coffee, a few fleeting moments each day before the reality of this shit world reasserted itself.

Mal pulled the prayer shawl off his head and straightened it over his shoulder before glancing at the man, nodding his acknowledgment.

"The wagon for the white man's bank comes today, early, from the southern road. It will leave before the sun reaches its highest point. Pahninee says you plan on robbing it."

"He isn't wrong."

"Is that why you make war on the evil spirits? For money and gold?"

"Nah, I've had plenty of both, and I suppose they're nice enough." He turned to face the young man. "No, it isn't about getting, it's about denying. While the Mallikim are serving Risti because he has power, the people are serving whoever is lining their pockets. You take out the banks, you take away their bread and butter, soon enough, they start to tear themselves apart. It'll crush the soul of this town." He saw the man wasn't following everything; he hadn't any idea about the Greek priest or the demons that had escaped the box. His understanding was steeped in his own mythology and the colonizers who took his land. "Already shut down their mines and ability to make more money. Next, I take out the money they already made."

The native didn't understand. He had been conditioned to expect the worst of those who came from beyond the sea, and Mal couldn't say that he blamed him. But he didn't need the Paiute to understand why he was doing what he was doing. He had asked for help, and they had denied it. He would discover his own path forward. Three more demons to kill, and by his count, he was only a quarter to his promised haul for Agrat. He had known how disgusting the work was going to be, but he hadn't realized how tedious. Castrating a hundred men, living and dead, was wearing on him, eating up his time. He nodded his thanks to the scout and whistled for Mishpat. It was time to go. He had to get back to Brodie and cut off the wagon before it could reach town. No time to waste on niceties.

NO GUILT OF BLOODSHED

It took longer than he had expected to get back to town, and for a bit he was worried he would miss the wagon entirely. As it was, he saw the dust kicked up by wagon wheels along the road as he came up on the south end of Brodie. Mal brought his horse to a stop, taking the time to check his gun was loaded and tying his tallit over his mouth and nose. Then he was off, riding hard down the dirt road, a cloud of darkness in the dust that rose behind him. He rode like a soul escaped from Sheol fleeing the damning angels. His eyes locked on the wagon ahead of him.

There was a driver and a shotgunner. Mal needed to deal with the gunner first. He rode hard as the horse allowed, but he could feel its pained breathing; he could see the blood in the foam flecked drool that fell from its mouth. He didn't need it to survive. He didn't need anything to survive this place. He would leave it as dead as the Priest had left his brother. He pushed the horse harder.

Riding up alongside the wagon, Mal pulled his pistol and grinned his hateful grin. He could shoot the shotgunner, take out the threat. But instead, he aimed at the lead wagon horse. His goal was not to be safe; his goal was to kill as many as he could as quickly as he could. He squeezed the trigger, but before the shot went off, something exploded from the wagon and slammed into him. Wood shrapnel filled the air around him as Mal was thrown from his horse and crashed into the dirt. He lay there dazed for a moment before rolling on to his hands and knees. He was about to stand when a boot connected with his ribs and sent him rolling over the ground. He pushed himself up off the dirt when a savage backhand caught him across the cheek and spun him around. He lost his balance and crashed into the brush beside the road.

Mal gasped for breath, feeling his left eye swelling shut and the blood trickling from his ear. A dark shadow resolved itself over him. It wasn't a completely human shape—two legs, two arms, a head, sure, but all the limbs bent at crooked and unnatural angles. The figure above him looked down with disappointed but amused eyes. They glowed a sickly green, like they were infecting the world around them. The figure lifted its boot and brought it down, pinning Malechai in place.

"Well, you're nothing if not predictable. Malechai ben Palache. Nothing, if not predictable." The 'man' leaned down. He was a slender, horrible man with a wide smile full of sharp teeth and swirling orbs of fireflies and other insects for eyes hidden behind small round spectacles. Malechai grabbed the leg that was on his chest and tried lifting it, failing. When the demon spoke, its voice was light and lilting, almost playful.

"I know that you're doing what you're doing for Agrat, we all know. We all know her little deal." He clicked his forked tongue against his teeth. "Now, it isn't often that someone gets as far into their end of the bargain as you have, very impressive, really. But it makes it very easy to follow you, doesn't it? Collecting the mutilated cocks of your enemies, leaving them sprawled all across town, the mines, and the whorehouse." The demon leaned forward, putting more weight on Mal's chest.

"I mean, really, as soon as Beliya'al found the corpses and discovered the Jews had fled, it was simple to connect the bloody dots to Agrat, and your stench is all over her. Hard to resist her, isn't it? Or was it? Did you pause and think to yourself who you were about to fuck? A demon, an inhuman thing? I'm sure your little scrolls say something about that, don't they?"

"Never gave it much thought," Malechai hissed through clenched teeth. It was hard to breathe through the pressure the demon was putting on his chest.

"No? Did you think about who else she has serviced with those lips and that body? Who else has enjoyed her? *What* else has enjoyed her? How do you think you rank against the bodies of malleable mallikim? How can you satisfy the woman who gave lay with the bull in Minos?" The man laughed loudly. "No matter what your god has blessed you with, you can never match the sheer adaptability of our kind. What could you possibly offer a woman like that?"

"Imagination," Malechai grunted in response, unable to keep himself from being a smartass, even with the sword of Damocles hanging above his head. "Women like creativity more than they like shitty lays, no matter how big the dick is." Mal reached up and gave the demon's upper thigh a solid punch, digging his knuckles into the meat.

The demon yowled as Mal's knuckles bruised the head of his festering flesh, and he pulled his leg back only to lash out with another kick that sent Malechai skidding across the ground. "Your stench and the stench of those you have killed. Finding her, taking her, enjoying her is all child's play for beings like us." The demon roared as it stalked towards Malechai again, reaching down to grab his jacket and pressing him into the dirt, his writhing insect eyes inches away from Mal's. He gestured with his head towards the now very dead horse that had been carrying his bags. "I could smell the deceased and rotting sex of humans from the bank. I knew you would want to draw me out, rob the stagecoach, bring me into an ambush. Me! Mammon, into an ambush." The demon shook its head. "You are so simple, driven to vengeance, a perfectly human specimen. Driven towards bloodshed and the promise of riches and fucking. Driven yet predictable."

Mammon's arm snaked out and caught Mishpat as the homunculus hound leapt for the demon's throat. Without breaking eye contact with Malechai, the demon slammed the creature into the ground and then flung it aside before returning the hand to Malechai's chest.

"That predictability I have learned from working the books of your banks, weighing the worth of a human life one coin and one murder at a time, you disgusting biological sack of waste. And now you lie here, in my grasp, about to be buried in the dirt and sand like your ancestors in Israel that I swallowed and shat into the filth so long ago. Mere fecal nothingness left behind. And Agrat will learn her place too, I promise you that. Once I finish with you, I'll join Beliya'al in punishing her. I'll show her just how imaginative I can be." He growled the last bit, savoring the flavor of his words on his lips before he stood and began walking back towards the nearly destroyed wagon he had burst from.

Malechai scrambled to his feet and drew his gun, desperate to stop the demon. There was a deafening bang. Smoke rose from the barrel of the pistol Mammon held. He had turned, drawn, and fired within the space of a heartbeat. He hadn't even taken the time to aim. But he never missed, he never misfired. A perfect shot through the heart of the Jewish stranger who would have happily killed all the demons. Malechai lay on his back once more, the hole in his shirt still smoking. "Predictable to the last, Malechai." He chuckled and turned back, heading for the wagon again. This had been too simple, too easy. Baladan had been a weakling to fall to such a pathetic mortal.

Before Mammon could reach the coach of the wagon, there was a second, hateful bang. At Mammon's feet, a hundred centipedes and fireflies writhed, baking on the hot ground, leaking from the exit wound that had, seconds ago, been the right side of his face. Two more shots rang out, the first tearing through the shotgunner's ribs, the second taking out the driver before he could spur his horses on. Mammon stood there, stunned and dumbfounded, his quivering, numb fingers prodding at the hole in his skull as he attempted to force the insects back in. Malechai didn't take chances. He walked up behind the demon and blew his gun arm in half, firing at point blank against the bone of his thin elbow.

Moving around in front of the demon, he reached into his breast pocket and lifted a silver disk with the image of the Chinese war god, Guan Yu, engraved on it. The bullet Mammon had fired hadn't even punctured the metal. "Maybe less predictable than you thought. Suppose saving those children earned me a bit of luck, or maybe allowing for their use drained you of yours. There's a balance in all things; you should know that, Mammon. You balanced the books of greed and fear for so long, you forgot what their absence looked like."

Gaping, his mouth working in silence, trying to form words, Mammon grasped out towards Malechai, who swatted the hand away with his gun. Malechai thought for a moment and then brought his sword out, giving it a few test swings, remembering the feel and weight of the blade in his hands. Satisfied, he looked up and met the slowly hollowing eye socket that remained whole in Mammon's head.

"I learned the hard way from Baladan. If I want to deliver the dick to Agrat, I can't banish you first. This will probably not be a terribly fun experience for you, Mammon, but at least, unlike those two," he jerked his head in the direction of the two dead men by the wagon, "you won't be left here in the sun to rot."

CHAPTER NINE
. . . AND BECAME AS DEAD MEN

BACK IN BRODIE, the line of deputies watched the dust cloud along the road into town growing larger. They were men. Men who served a thing. If it rankled them to be in the service of a monster, none of them dared voice that concern. The men were all members of Saint Cyprian's church. They had all been inducted into the inner circle and exposed to the true nature of their sheriff. Beliya'al was an angel, a divine being, one of four that had been given power in Brodie. It was the reason the town was so successful, why they found such prosperity.

Some of those inducted into the order and blessed by Father Risti went mad. They couldn't handle the holy truths bestowed on them by the Greek priest. But those who were able to accept the divine nature of their visitors, they were blessed and given an even greater share of the material blessings than most the common folk of Brodie. Of course, it had also been explained to them that the conception of a kind and loving God was a myth, only followers of the true faith, good Christians who attended the correct church, should be afforded respect, all others must serve.

If that sat wrong with any of the deputies, they were smart enough not to put voice to it. But the truth was that the power dynamic they were handed, the money, the women, it made whatever moral qualms they had evaporate. How could it be wrong? Sure, the priest's faith was different than that touted by the dour brimstone preachers who traveled around preaching for coin in whatever city would allow it. But Risti was a priest, and he was served by angels. Wasn't that proof enough that they were on the side of righteousness?

Earlier in the day, the banker had come in and spoken to the sheriff in hushed tones. The smile that so often graced his fat face and thin lips melted away, and he left to go enact some holy plan. So sure were the deputies of the divine nature of not only their masters, but of their mission, that they didn't question it when the sheriff had come into the jail dragging the struggling whore behind him. They had all wondered at that. Would they take turns? Was he keeping her for himself? But that was answered almost immediately when he sent them away. There was a madman on the loose. The one from the saloon, the one murdering men and cutting off their cocks. Beliya'al had let him live that day in the saloon. But he was no longer amused by the killer. Something had changed. Something had happened that drained the laughter from their gluttonous master.

He had commanded his deputies to wait at the edge of town, to be prepared for the maniac to attack in broad daylight! With the dust kicked up by the wagon heading into town, it was flying down the road like a bat escaping the fires of hell. It was unlikely that any sane man, any man that meant good by the people of Brodie, would be driving the horses that fast and that hard. But that was the sum of it, wasn't it? They served the angels. This killer, this Jew, served the diabolic powers. Good vs. Evil, and they full-heartedly believed they were on the right side.

The deputies flanked the road into town, side to a side, watching the wagon's mad approach into town. The horses foamed at the mouth, their breath coming in terrible ragged gasps as they fled in terror from whatever came behind. The lawmen raised their guns and took aim at the wagon. If the Jew thought he could get the drop on them by riding in the wagon, he was going to be in for a serious lead filled surprise. The deputies were simple men, flesh and blood, but they had seen strange things in the days since the priest and his angels had come into town, they had been hardened by the sights and sounds in St. Cyprian's little cathedral. Too hardened to spook at the sight of horses charging down the road. But damn it all, the wagon was moving fast, too fast. As it approached, they could see a hole had been blasted out the side. Almost on instinct, the men on the right side of the road took aim at the hole.

Gunshot and smoke filled the sky of Brodie as the deputies opened fire, fanning cylinders and pouring their bullets into the interior of the wagon. It was only through a miracle of their patron's doing that they didn't hit one another. The speed of the wagon and fury of their ambush was such that the deputies couldn't get a good look in the hole in the wagon. They couldn't make out the long, lanky torso of Mammon in the shadows. They couldn't see that his limbs had been cut off and arranged next to his body or the two severed heads that had been placed, open-mouthed, next to the bloody torso's crotch, catching the angelic blood that still pumped from the wound that was there instead of its twisted, malformed cock. They couldn't see the fear and rage in the creature's face as they fired shot after shot into his body.

So intent were they on filling the wagon with lead as it rushed by and down the street. They didn't notice what dropped from between the wheels.

Malechai fell to the ground between the wheels of the wagon and watched as it passed over him. Now on his back, a pistol gripped in each fist, he opened fire. Now, Mal was a fantastic shot, but from his awkward position, it wasn't as easy to hit those kill shots, and he didn't trust he had the surplus of time to waste, and so many of his shots went wide of the mark, but he was still about the business of murder. At first, the deputies had no idea what the hell was happening. They were still shooting at the wagon, so Mal's gunshots didn't register. No one even noticed when the first deputy fell back, clutching at his throat as he tried to stop the blood gushing from the wound, or the next man who collapsed with a slug in his gut. It wasn't until Joseph, the biggest and meanest deputy's head exploded in a mess of skull and brains that anyone took notice that someone was firing back at them. They watched the stub of his neck as the tongue flapped around wildly before he collapsed.

Several still fired on the wagon, not realizing that their advantage was quickly disintegrating. As the horses finally collapsed, done in by the mix of exhaustion, over-exertion, and bullet wounds, the wagon crashed onto its side, spilling the mutilated body of the banker from its innards, along with the two free rolling heads. By the time the deputies realized they were being shot, it was too late for all but three of the men. The target of their vengeance had finally presented, and they had all wasted their bullets on the wagon.

Mal rolled onto his stomach and popped off the ground to his feet, dropping the pistols and pulling out the shotgun he had stolen from the wagon-rider. He brought it to bear and pressed the barrels against the chest of the oncoming deputy. The man didn't have time to be afraid as Mal depressed both triggers and sent him flying across the street with a pulped chest, shards of ribs protruding from the slop of his torso like the jagged teeth of a rabid dog. Mal turned towards the next man who was rushing to meet him. He pulled his finger from the trigger guard and gripped the stock before swinging the shotgun like a club and clobbering the man in the face with the metal barrel. He swung hard enough to warp the barrel, sending the man staggering back to collapse in a boneless heap.

Before Mal could get his bearing, the third deputy

tackled him to the ground, already swinging low, quick punches into his side. Mal's sides ached, still bruised and cracked from his scuffle with the banker. The two men rolled across the ground, each trying to fight dirty, each trying to force the other to submit. As they came to a stop, the deputy, a large man with a scraggly pube beard and yellowed teeth, smiled triumphantly and began raining blows down on Mal's face. Mal struggled to block the punches and then grabbed the man's wrists as his hands wrapped around Mal's throat and squeezed.

Mal gritted his teeth, his vision blurring as air and blood was denied to his brain. The deputy was stronger. Mal flailed, kicking his legs, trying to buck the man off of him. The man was heavy, at least two hundred pounds of muscle under one hundred pounds of fat. His hands were stubby but large enough to circle his throat. Mal grasped blindly, trying to get his hands on any weapon he could find. He felt the pulpy mess of the chest from the man he had shot with the shotgun. His hand sunk into the morass of his chest cavity. Mal's hand whipped out of the man's chest and slammed into his assailant's throat, stabbing the broken off shard of rib deep into the deputy's neck. Not letting go, Mal twisted the rib, digging through the meat of the deputy with the bone of another man. The ragged edges of shattered bone cut and gouged, and blood geysered from between the torn skin and the bone, coating Malechai's hand. The deputy wasn't strangling him anymore; he was weakly grabbing at his throat. But Mal didn't stop; he continued his gristly work of tearing his throat apart.

Finally, the mountain of a man fell to the side. Mal lay still for a moment, trying to catch his breath. A shadow fell over him, and his blurred vision was filled with the sight of a colt revolver aimed at his skull. Behind the revolver, the man he had clubbed with the shotgun smiled an ugly smile.

"I got you, you cock sucking sack of shit. I got you dead to rights." He was gleeful. He wasn't thinking of the horror of telling eleven families that their menfolk were dead. He wasn't thinking of the horror show Malechai had wrought. He thought only of his own glory. He was the hero; he was the conqueror. And though he didn't know this yet, he was already dead. "You got any last words?"

"Yeah." Mal's scarred face stretched into its own smile, a horrible leer that seemed as evil as it was dismissive. "*Sic 'em.*"

The deputy didn't have time to wonder what the enigmatic phrase might have meant. Mishpat, who had hidden within the shadows of the wagon, emerged at a full run and lunged. His leap carried him high. He grabbed the man by the throat, dragging him down to the ground. The man screamed in pain and fear as the man-made mastiff shook him like a bit of rope, snapping his neck rather quickly. But Mishpat kept shaking, kept chewing, tearing the head clean off. Malechai ignored the display, pulling himself off the ground, retrieving his gun, and reloading as he walked towards the wagon, towards Mammon's still living body.

Mal stepped past the quivering demonic flesh of the banker and grabbed the saddlebags with his belongings and the bounty that he had tucked into the wagon. He whistled, calling the mastiff. The dog-like creature grunted and looked down at his plaything; other than being wrapped in bloodied and torn flannel, it was hardly recognizable as a human corpse now. It didn't want to leave its toy, but the creature trotted over and allowed Mal to set the saddlebags on its back.

"Good boy." Mal grinned, scratching the golem behind the ear before turning his attention to the bloodied demon. The torso and head sat there, radiating hatred and pain. He had cut off the creature's limbs and castrated him before gagging him with his own severed dick and setting him in the wagon. Now his body was perforated by dozens of bullets and buck, as well as wooden shrapnel that had been blasted from the wagon. All in all, it was a disgusting and pitiful site. Mal reached forward and pulled the shriveled manhood from the demon's throat and set it on the ground. Mammon made croaking sounds, attempting to form words around the tattered remains of his lips, few remaining teeth, and punctured lungs.

"Shhh," Mal admonished as he pulled out his shofar and the Chinese charms, he spoke as he placed several of the charms on the banker's body. "When I blow this horn, Sheriff'll know that you are dead. Just like the whole town of Brodie has seen this, no more skulking in the shadows. No more hiding. I assume I'll have to go to that fat ass ball of shit you call a sheriff, though. Even called out as you are, ain't not one of you willing to step forward to the challenge. You are so used to intimidating Christians and them running and hiding, you forgot. You and yours are imperfect, Mallikim, you and yours were made to be extinguished."

Mal watched the demon's eyes dispassionately as he brought the ram's horns to his twisted lips and blew a single note that shattered the air around them. Finally, Mammon found the power to make sound, and he screamed as his flesh bubbled. Huge boils appeared and popped in blood filled bursts, the blood boiling away and evaporating in the air as the demon melted. His skin went first, then his muscles; his rolling hate-filled eyes set in a gold-plated skull was the last thing to dissolve into the demonic sludge that would be the only thing to mark his ever having existed. Mal regretted that; a solid golden skeleton would fetch a pretty price, no matter where he was. But it was done. Mal stood and looked back at the street filled with corpses. He needed to harvest, but every moment he hesitated was a moment Agrat was in the hands of Beliya'al. He couldn't say why, but that irked him something fierce. Perhaps the succubus had gotten her claws into his heart after all, foul sheydim magics. Nothing for it now, he would have to deal with that after he killed the final law man in Brodie.

"Mishpat," he called, getting the golem's attention. He gestured to the bodies lying all over the road. "Fetch." Joyously, Mishpat went to work, tearing bodies apart to do his master's bidding. Mal nodded and turned to walk towards the jailhouse but was surprised by a single man standing in his path.

The man was dressed in somber threadbare blacks and held a crucifix in one hand, outstretched like a weapon. The man trembled and quaked in his boots; sweat plastered his hair, thinning as it was, to his scalp.

"You'll come no further, demon! The power of Christ compels you to leave the good people of Brodie!" His arm trembled as he thrust the crucifix towards Malechai.

"What are you doing, old man?" Mal asked, walking forward calmly. He hadn't seen this side of Christianity, nor this kind of priest before.

"I am Reverend Obediah Bartly, and I demand you quit this place!" Even his voice quivered. But he believed, Mal could tell, that his cross and his conviction would somehow drive Malechai off. He continued, stepping forward to meet Malechai on the road. "Oh, heavenly father, defend us in our battle against the principalities and powers, against the rulers of the world of darkness, and against the spirits of wickedness in high places! In the name of Jesus Christ, our God and Lord, we confidently undertake to repulse and rebuke the attacks of the devil! God arises—" He yelped in pain as Mal reached forward and closed his fist around the outstretched hand and twisted the man's hand painfully.

One handed, he continued to twist the man's hand in his crushing grip, forcing Reverend Obediah to one knee. "What are you talking about, you old fool?" He withdrew his revolver and rested the barrel against the man's forehead, just between the eyes.

"I am exorcising you! I will protect the people of this town!" he exclaimed, wincing with every ounce of pressure Mal asserted on him. "You are a murderous demon, and you will be ended by Jesus Chri—" His eyes bugged out as Mal twisted sharply, nearly breaking the man's wrist.

"You think I am the demon?" It was almost amusing, the evil that these people saw while ignoring the evil that was convenient. It would be more amusing if not for the smoldering ruins of the synagogue he had visited just yesterday.

"You *are* a demon, a monster who has come to town dripping with hate and malice and disdain for our Lord Jesus Christ!"

"Well, three out of four of those." Malechai nodded. "But I'm no monster, least not how you—"

"Lies! You are death, who comes scythe in hand!"

"No!" Malechai suddenly shouted, raising his gun to point at the silhouette of the cross with its three crossbars that stood against the blistering skies above the town. "You welcomed Death on his pale horse, hooves dripping with the blood of my people as he rode into town. You laid palms at his feet and crowned him a prince. You welcomed death . . . " Mal met the preacher's eyes. "I am merely that which follows after."

He brought the gun back down and placed it against the holy man's knee before pulling the trigger and obliterating the man's kneecap. Mal rose, he dripped gore. He looked down without pity at the reverend, who rolled in the dirt screaming, clutching what was left of his leg.

"Mishpat!"

The mastiff paused in the gruesome work of tearing genitals from bodies to look to its master.

"This one too," Mal commanded, and then continued on his path towards the jail house.

CHAPTER TEN
JUSTICE, JUSTICE YOU SHALL PURSUE

NO ONE ELSE stepped into Malechai's path as he made his approach to the jail. Not one erstwhile preacher or lawman. No miners, no shopkeeps, no guards. No one wanted to get in his way. Windows locked and doors were barred at his passing. He had left the realm of secretly causing mayhem far behind. There was no element of surprise. He was sure the deranged priest watched him from some window in his ugly church. He wondered if Dragan recognized him, if Dragan understood that retribution for his crimes in Europe had come. That no matter how far into the desert of the untamed lands of the American West he fled, Malechai would hunt him down.

Mal tipped his hat towards the church; he would come back soon enough for it. But first, he had to extricate Agrat from the situation she found herself in and end the sheriff. He couldn't even enter the unholy ground that the priest called his church until he had dealt with two more demons. But he was aware that it may not be all that easy. Each demon had given him more trouble than the last; he had barely survived his tussle with Mammon. And at the mines, there had been a swarm of lesser demons among the humans; who knew how many lesser shit fuckers he would have to tear through before he got to the last two?

Malechai paused at the door of the jailhouse. He stepped to the side, not wanting to be shot as soon as he opened the door, and kicked it open with his foot. No gunshots sounded. Carefully, Mal stepped around to peer inside the jailhouse. He took a step back, overwhelmed by the unexpected sight of a visa of canyons and black chasms that existed beyond the door—another land, another sky, another world just beyond the doorstop. From somewhere among the shadows of those caves and monolithic stones, the sheriff's voice called out.

"We're in here, boy. You are welcome to join us."

Behind his words, Mal thought he could hear the muffled screams of a woman with a gag in her mouth. Agrat. He considered the succubus for a moment; he owed her nothing beyond the collection of the phalli as his part of the bargain. But he had seen in her eyes, seen the rage and pain that felt so in sync with his own. She had been a prisoner, had been at the mercy of these other creatures for as long as she could remember. To leave her to that fate would be tantamount to leaving the Jews of Brodie locked in their homes waiting for death. Perhaps she was manipulating him even now. But he couldn't ignore the fear and pain in the muffled moans he had heard. He stepped past the doorway into that alien landscape beyond.

It was impossibly warm within this new realm. The sun, angry and red, hung above in the sky, baking the hard packed red dirt underneath. Despite the sun overhead, shadows dominated the landscape, cast at impossible angles from cliffs, dead trees, and stone monuments carved in shapes that hurt Malechai's eyes to look at.

Malechai looked back the way he had come. Standing there, unnatural in its surroundings, was the door. Through the cracks in the door, he could see the main street of Brodie. It was his way back, if he should survive this trip into whatever strange realm Beliya'al had brought him to. Malechai turned back towards the desolate desert vista and snarled at the wrongness of it. In the air, buzzards with three legs and four heads circled. Things that looked like scorpions crossbred with centipedes hissed and clicked as they scurried over the sand. Even the clouds looked wrong. Tinted red from the sun, they seemed to swirl and reform into obscene shapes even as they sat frozen in the sky.

Almost despite himself, a mumbled prayer fell from Mal's lips. Not that he thought the holy one, blessed be, would do shit in this situation. Mal had learned long ago that if you needed something, you could pray all you want, but unless you were willing to get your hands bloody, you would never get shit. Mal's hands were plenty bloody. This wasn't the first time he had visited terror on a town; he had made a living as a monster. But Brodie was proving to test even his prodigious capacity for violence. That and normally he wasn't alone; normally he had his siblings with him. Sibling, now.

He stepped forward, finally moving deeper into the strange hell-scape that existed within Brodie's jail house. The only path forward was a path through the canyon, a shadowed foreboding chasm that cut through the jagged stones and was plunged into shadow. As soon as foot set to the darkness between the canyon faces, the stifling heat of the unnatural sun faded and gave way to a grotesque chill. It wasn't simply cold. It was the frozen pain that reached the bones and the soul. It was the feeling of being in that prison in the frozen wastes of the Ukraine once more. It was the mind-numbing experience of watching your brother die of exposure while awaiting a judgment that would never come before the sentence was carried out.

Mal pulled his duster closer around himself, trying to stave off the supernatural cold that existed within the shadows. But the cold wasn't the only thing that made the darkness in those deep cracks and caves home. Things skittered in the darkness, clacking mandibles that dripped caustic blood. Mal kept his eyes straight forward, ignoring the horrific insects and things sheltering from the hateful sun above. They were thriving in the icy winds of the chasm. Canines that were constructed entirely out of human teeth and misshapen things that moaned from multiple mouths that wore human skulls in place of clothes. They reached for him, gibbering wordless pleas and threats from broken mouths. Mal touched the grip of his revolver, comforting himself as much as warning the grasping things away.

They were converging behind him. Getting closer. A promise within the nonsense babble of their words that he would join them, that this would be his home and they, his family. But Mal had a family. Mal didn't need a home. He only had one need, and it couldn't be answered by the braying and madness to be found in the cliffs of this realm. It would be answered by finding the master of this place and putting a bullet between his eyes. With this determination, Mal pushed through the dark places and pulled from the rotting grasps of things that had once been men before making bargains with damned things. Finally, he walked out the other side of the chasm, out of the darkness and back into the broiling sun. The whimpers and shrieks of those behind him assured him the things were fleeing back into the safety of their icy prison and would not follow.

Before him stretched a long cobblestone road wet with blood. Like a river, it flowed down over his boots and broke to either side of the canyons. In the thick stream of vitae floated chunks of meat and discernible pieces of people. An eye here, a nose there, fingers and toes and globs of flesh all floated in the flow of blood. Looking down the bloody road, Mal laid eyes on the origin of the bloody river. A jailhouse. A jail within a jail, but this one was here for him. It wasn't the Brodie jailhouse, no, this particular prison had a corollary in the real world. His brother had died in this prison. Mal's lips peeled back away from his teeth in a disgusted snarl. It was a cheap trick from a desperate devil. One that he would not be dissuaded by. He started up the path.

No Guilt of Bloodshed

The Sheriff's voice thundered out over the sound of Mal's boots, catching in the thick clotting river. "You come this far, boy? I told you I was bored, and oh! How you deliver, boy!" His accent was strange, an odd conglomeration of French and the thick soup of southern dialect Mal had grown used to here. "You killed Mammon and Baladan. You must think you're on a roll, that you got all the cards on your side and that you are a step away from victory." The demon's laughter boomed so loud across the landscape that the very earth shook, spreading ripples across the bloody river.

Decaying and rotting hands shot up from the thin stream of blood, emerging from the fluid as though it were deeper than it was. Mal drew his cavalry sword but continued to stalk forward. All along the stretching path towards the jail, the dead were emerging from the blood. He recognized some of the dead, the deputies he had shot down in the street just inside an hour ago. They moaned his name, all of them. They grabbed at him, only to be met with the slicing edge of his blade as he cut his way through the dead as though they were mere vines. They crowded around him, the dead and rotting faces of foes he had put in the ground.

They parted, revealing Mal's brother, Yitzak. He was emaciated and hollow. *"You walk the river of blood you have spilled, facing the victims you have murdered, and it doesn't even slow you,"* Yitzak mocked in Yiddish. His voice was like the ice wind of the chasm Mal had left behind, and it cut him to the bone.

"I've never been one to live in the past, Azi," Mal said, pushing past his dead brother to continue.

The dead flanked the bloody pathway on either side, a processional of the violence Malechai had brought into the world. He ignored the faces of the men and women he had murdered. Some on the battlefield, some in their homes while they were sleeping. Others he didn't recognize. It was to be expected when you had steeped your life in bloody deeds as Malechai had. But something bothered him.

"Why are you here, Azi? I didn't kill you. I loved you."

"Hah! You deceive yourself still?" Yitzak grinned, revealing blood flecked teeth that had cracked while he had spasmed in the throes of death. *"You killed me, as surely as if you had slit my throat. You were the one who demanded we protect the people."*

"They were our people, Azi. We couldn't do nothing."

"Why not? You have done nothing for people plenty of times. You have left the innocent to die, why does them being Jews matter to you? Ah, because suddenly it did. Whatever happened in Spain, you came back changed. You wanted to retire, to find a wife and settle down. You! Bloody Malechai, the Killer of Cardova, the Wraith of Wallachia, the Butcher of Brodie."

Mal paused at that last title, shooting Yitzak a raised eyebrow and a scowl. *"No one calls me that."*

"What do you think they'll call you after this? The Mohel?" Yitzak returned.

Mal grunted. Yitzak, or the thing wearing Yitzak's face, had a point there. *"Nothing wrong with wanting to settle down, to see an end to the blood."*

"It isn't who you are, Mal; it has never been who you are, or who you will be! If you hadn't brought us to that town, tried to get us to settle with you, even as you saw the rising hatred towards the Jews, if you hadn't played at being a good man, we would have either left or murdered the Christians in their sleep. Either way, I would be alive."

Mal whirled on the ghost of his brother and his accusations. *"You think I don't know that, Azi? You think I don't carry that knowledge in my heart? But I am tired, Azi, dead fucking tired. And every bullet I put into one of these . . . "* he gestured to the parade of dead around him, *"is just one closer to me feeding myself one. I may not be a good man, maybe I shouldn't have pretended to be."* Mal closed his eyes, steeling himself against the pain in his chest and remembering his purpose. *"But I'm responsible for no man but myself. That includes you, Azi."*

When Mal opened his eyes again, the dead were gone. Yitzak was gone, and he was alone on the dusty dry cobblestone path up to the jail. Mal sheathed his sword and continued his hike.

"Not even family matters, not to you. That's impressive!" The thick sludge drawl of the Sheriff's voice boomed over the landscape again. "You done so good killing Baladan and Mammon, you think you invincible now, boy! But you ain't. Them was malikim and sheydim, simple little spirits and half-formed things that play at being mighty. I was there when this world was born!" The earth shook under Malechai, and glittering towers of ivory and gold burst from the ground around the jail. An entire city of white and sapphire. "It was me and my brothers that brought you pitiful things the gifts you have. We brought you magic and violence and beauty. We taught you our ways. That one you pray to was happy to leave you to your own devices, but me and mine, we watched you, and we wanted to elevate you."

All over the towers and buildings that had burst from the ground like weeds jutting from the ground, eyes opened, great, terrible eyes that wept blood and mucus and stared down at Malechai with hate.

Beliya'al continued, his voice echoing across the broken landscape. "You got the mark of Azazel on you, boy, you marked, and you carry him glory wherever you go. But you a man, and I'm Grigori, ain't no way this end the way you want it to."

Malechai ignored the taunting, the mind-churning gaze of the towers, and made it to the door of the jail. He kicked it in and stepped inside.

The interior of the building inside the realm of madness that the fallen angel had crafted was unexpected. Malechai had expected some grand, torturous chamber, something out of a nightmare. But he found himself standing in a normal jail, dusty, muggy in the stifling oven air of a building that baked in the Brodie sun. There was a cell built into one corner of the small room and a desk scooted against the wall. In the center of the room, the bloated toad-thing Beliya'al stood waiting for him. He looked ridiculous in the ill-fitting clothes. He looked like a horrible, spoiled sausage that was splitting the casing. Next to him, tied to a chair, Agrat sat, her hair matted to her face. Blood ran from her nose and one ear. Her lip had been busted in some struggle as well and was leaking blood onto the fabric that had been shoved down her throat to act as a gag.

Malechai stood across the room from the two of them, taking in the scene, knowing now that this thing wearing the skin of a sheriff was an unholy divine being, a creature that broke sync with natural order and a renegade against God. It should have had more of an impact than it did. But Malechai had seen the same unkindness, the same swagger, and the same weakness in these things as he had seen in men his whole life. There was nothing special, holy, or unholy about these things. Power didn't earn his respect, no matter where that power came from or what it was.

"I come for you, Beliya'al," Malechai said, pulling his gun from his belt and holding it loosely at his side.

"You do, you do. I grant you that. But because you do such a good job of making this place more interesting, I make you a deal."

Malechai's eyes narrowed as he watched the corrupted sheriff step towards Agrat.

"I know how you like making deals, so here is your deal: you get to live, I break the wards over that there church, you do your business, you leave." Beliya'al's great slimy tongue poked from between his lips and licked his chin, leaving a long trail of mucus there. As it withdrew into his mouth, several eyes opened on it and stared at Malechai.

"And what do you want in exchange for that bargain?"

Mal asked, his eyes glued to the disgusting glistening patch of skin where the angel had licked.

"Oh, nothing you can't pay, boy. You just leave me an' Agrat here is all you gotta do. You made this fun for me; you get to leave here and go to tend your business with Dragan. I break all the seals for you. You ain't even got to try your hand at killing the old bitch, which, between you and me, you ain't got no chance against, anyway. See, you was doomed to fail, 'tween me and Tanin'iver, you was fuckin' doomed. This deal, this deal is your only way to see your revenge."

"You want . . . Agrat." Malechai repeated, "Why is she worth more to you than stopping me?"

"Ah, she ain't. She ain't worth shit, but she's worth more than a human woman. See, human women, they break real easy. They break and they dead and all the fun you can have making new holes to fuck with new things is done. Agrat here, she can't die. She can't escape the fun. Centuries of fun and imagination to be had. You known her one night, Jew; I'll know her for one thousand before I even repeat an act."

"And if I refuse your deal?" Malechai pressed.

"Then you fucking die and I still get to fuck every natural and unnatural hole I can create in Agrat for eternity, and your priest gets to lord over Brodie and continue to spread his willpower across the land! Think, boy, this ain't even a question. On one hand, you get everything you fucking want; on the other, you die trying to save the virtue of a whore. You can't banish me like you did with the others. There is nothing you can do that will hurt . . . " He paused as the sounds of a door opening came from behind Malechai.

Malechai did not turn to see what it was.

Mishpat padded into the jail, trotting slowly between the angel, the demon, and the Jew. He glanced at Beliya'al and turned to Malechai and horked once before vomiting at Malechai's feet. All three were silent as they watched the golem in effigy of a hound vomit nearly a score of severed, ragged, and torn dicks onto the wooden floor of the jail. Agrat made a satisfied muffled laugh, and Malechai smirked as the final penis, pale with golden filigree tattooed onto it, fell onto the pile.

"Good boy," Malechai praised the hound before lifting his gun and firing. Even as he lifted the weapon, Beliya'al was moving, charging towards him.

"You missed, Jew!" the angel roared as he grabbed Malechai off the floor and lifted him, his mouth opening impossibly wide. From inside Beliya'al's mouth, hundreds of eyes and smaller mouths opened, each focused on Mal or screaming his crimes at him in high-pitched, hateful voices. As Beliya'al's fingers dug into his arm, Malechai dropped his gun, the pain too much to keep a good grip. The angel's blinking slimy tongue unfurled from the depth of that wide mouth and emerged, covered in suckers, smaller mouths, and eyes. It lapped against Mal's face, biting and whispering as it passed, and then wrapped around Malechai. He dangled there in the air for a moment before the tongue lashed and threw him into the bars of the cell.

In that same moment, the angel spun, lashing out with one stubby grotesque leg and smashed Mishpat into the desk. The angel lifted a hand and made a strange sign in the air, something shimmered in the space between the hound and angel, and then Mishpat's flesh begin to bubble and morph, soft clay in the creative hands of the angelic monster.

Malechai struggled to his feet, but he was moving slowly, still injured from his fight with Mammon and the deputies, and the angel was already there, sickly black wings stretching out behind his bloated body, filling the jail. He lifted Malechai by his throat, slamming him into the bars again and again. Malechai's head bounced off the iron, stars swum in his vision. Malechai laughed, he laughed so hard that the scars on his face threatened to tear open.

Beliya'al growled and pulled the Jew close to his face, the reek of rot and death heavy on his breath. "Why you laughing? You already lose your mind? Gone insane? We haven't even begun to play, boy!"

Malechai struggled to control his laughter, shaking his head. Then he dropped the facade, his smile dropping to the deadly sneer that almost always graced his face. "I didn't miss shit."

Beliya'al didn't have a chance to ponder what the little mortal meant before Agrat swung the chair she had formerly been chained to at the back of his head. With a howl of rage, Beliya'al dropped Malechai and turned to face this new threat. As he landed, Mal pulled his knife from his belt and leapt onto the sheriff's back, slamming the blade into the meat there again and again.

Agrat wrapped her long hands around the lashing tongue and pulled, dragging the angel forward, ignoring the tongue's teeth as they dug into her flesh. She lifted her leg and kicked the rotund creature in the chest, pushing him with all of her considerable might. Malechai continued to cut, his knife slicing through the rugged leather of the angel's flesh and sliding through thick layers of fat, but he couldn't seem to find an organ, or even bone, through the gristle of the angel's body. Black blood oozed from every hole, thick, sticky, and smelling of myrrh.

With a sickening ripping sound, Agrat pulled the writhing organ from Beliya'al's mouth, unrooting it and tossing it aside as the angel's mouth filled with more brackish blood. He gurgled his wordless bellows of pain and rage at them, shoving Agrat away and reaching over his back to grab Malechai to fling him towards the puddle of clay where Mishpat was reforming. Malechai slipped and pushed himself back up, finally pulling his sword out, his knife still lodged in the blubbery mass of the angel's back.

"That should shut you up," Agrat sneered. "You're so desperate to have at me with your little cock. Let's see it then." She stormed forward and swiped at Beliya'al, her fingers like talons tearing through clothes and flesh. Thick yellow globs of fat splattered across the floor of the jail, and black blood sprayed from his mouth as he screamed. Malechai held back as he watched Agrat hacking at the swiftly weakening angel.

"I am not your toy!" she screamed, her rage rising more as she continued to tear at him, ripping his skin from muscle and bone, great gobs of quivering flesh raining down in the wake of her attack. "I am not your thing!" She howled as she ripped his trousers away and gripped his balls in hands that had become vicious blood covered talons. "You will not touch me again!" she hissed as she ripped her hand away, shredding the skin of his angelic scrotum to tatters. The angel howled in agony and gritted his teeth, trying to stem the flow of blood.

Two testes, milky white and dripping with viscous black blood, dangled from the hole where his scrotum used to be. Agrat gripped them and ripped upwards, pulling the veins up as she slammed the testes against his mouth, straining them through his own teeth. She was panting, tears of rage marring her makeup as she shoved the sheriff back.

Mal stepped past her, raising his sword.

He didn't take his time; he didn't drag it out any more than he needed to. With every rise and fall of his arm, Malechai lopped off more of the angel until it lay in a hundred quivering pieces across the floor.

"Will that kill him?" he asked the succubus, who had retreated to the far wall of the jail to try to get control of her emotions, with little success.

Agrat looked up, seeming to remember Malechai was there for the first time since he had fired the bullet that had torn through her chains. She looked wild-eyed between the blood-soaked Jew and the chunks of lard and organs on the ground. She shook her head. "No . . . but it will keep him down for a while . . . maybe for long enough."

"Long enough." Malechai chuckled and used the tip of his sword to skewer what was left of Beliya'al's manhood. "Unlike this." He spat off to the side and kicked the organ off into the pile Mishpat had vomited earlier. He glanced at his hound, who was mostly reformed; the thing wagged pathetically, as if apologizing for not being more help. Mal shook his head, scratching the hound's half formed ear before grabbing the saddle bag and adding the regurgitated penises to his bounty. "If we're on a clock 'til he pulls himself back together, we should go."

"We?" Agrat asked suddenly, her dark eyes rising to meet his.

"You stay in town, you stay here, Risti's men will be after you again; better for you to come with me, stay safe 'til we get this sorted." Malechai clicked his tongue, summoning Mishpat to his side. The hound limped, as his limbs were still reforming, but dutifully took the burden of the saddlebags. Gathering up his dropped weapons, Mal rolled his neck, ready to face the trek back through hell to get to town. He opened the door and was surprised to see the dust and empty street of Brodie.

"Without his will and hatred sustaining it, we can't be held in his realm," Agrat said from behind him.

Malechai nodded, happy to be back on real, heaven created soil again.

"All right then," Mal murmured, "let's find a horse and get."

CHAPTER ELEVEN

. . . AND NOTHING YOU DESIRE COMPARES

MALECHAI MOVED QUICKLY, keeping his head down as best he could, nearly dragging Agrat by the arm as he rushed across the town of Brodie back towards her home. He needed a horse. He was covered in gore; the blood of men, angels, and demons saturated every garment. He was dripping with the crimes he had committed in Brodie. His eyes darted to every window and doorway. Both he and Agrat were in rough shape. Between Mammon and Beliya'al, he had taken one too many hits, fired one too many shots. Now he was out of stamina, ammo, and willpower. If someone should stop them or challenge them, he wasn't sure he would be able to come out on top.

So, he stuck to what few shadows he could find in the blistering brightness of the Brodie sun and moved as quickly as he could. He was sure they would be stopped, that there would be hundreds out looking for blood. He had left a trail of bodies from one end of the town to the other. Even for the few who hadn't lost a loved one in the destruction of the mines, they would have heard about the wanton death and castration of men within the confines of this blood-soaked city.

But then, the darkness that Dragan Risti had brought on the town was oppressive; the people were used to horrors here now. While Malechai had no knowledge of this, travesties were an everyday occurrence here. The sexual aberrations of the angel and the priest and the corruption of the town's institutions had soaked Brodie in blood and degeneracy. While Malechai had introduced an extreme level of violence and new flavors of fear and darkness to the city, the truth was that as soon as Risti had opened the doors of his church, Brodie had been damned. The very air was eroding the souls and willpower of those who would stand against darkness and lifting up those who would revel in it in equal measure.

Those few who did look from their windows and spot the blood drenched gun slinger dragging the beaten whore behind him either knew to mind their own damn business or were otherwise too self-absorbed to care. Either way worked for Malechai, and he breathed a sigh of relief as they got to the saloon and walked around back. There he was, the horse that Malechai had originally taken from the highwaymen. Mal pulled the saddlebags off of Mishpat and set them on the horse, stroking the beast's side to keep it calm. He glanced over his shoulder at Agrat. She was looking down. Her bruises and smeared makeup made her look a mess, a beautiful mess, like the sunrise over a battlefield. He frowned, his scars pulling painfully at his flesh, then he pulled himself onto the horse and offered her a hand.

"Come on."

She glanced up at him. She seemed unsure of herself, lost in her own thoughts. She looked conflicted but finally reached up and took his hand, allowing herself to be hauled up onto the horse behind him. Without another word, Malechai kicked the horse into a gallop, once again heading east out of town.

They rode in silence for hours. Agrat leaned forward, resting her head on his back, her arms lightly against his chest. He didn't know if she was crying, asleep, or still just zoning out from whatever had happened to her before he got to the jail. He thought of his sister. Ivanna and Agrat were both strong women, both taking what they wanted from the world without giving any quarter. But where Ivanna had Malechai and Yitzak watching over her, who did Agrat have? Being strong in this world wasn't enough. A lone figure, even a powerful predator, was soon prey when it had no one to watch its back. The world was many terrible things, a predator, a cesspool of violence, hatred, and bigotry. But it had never been lonely, not for him. But now Yitzak was dead, and his sister was on the other side of an impossibly large ocean.

Malechai felt terribly alone in that moment. He had been so absorbed in his mission of death for so long that he hadn't had time to mourn Yitzak; even on the boat, his mind was still fixed on vengeance. Mal didn't cry, didn't know that he could. But he hurt, the pain in his heart echoing his body. He had pushed himself beyond the natural limits of a human. And he wasn't done yet. He still had further to go.

Mal stopped the horse sometime later. The sun was dipping low over the horizon, and he knew that he would either be greeted or shot down momentarily. As if on cue, a single shot rang out, the bullet passing close enough to ruffle his beard. He didn't move, didn't even blink.

"What are you doing here, Winnemucca? Why are you back, and why do you bring evil with you?" The voice of Pahninee floated from the shadows, and once again, a group of the Paiute emerged from the brush and darkness, rifles leveled at him.

"We're hurt, all of us, town isn't safe for us anymore . . . "

"You were in good health when you left this morning, Winnemucca, and we let you leave that way. Why do you come back stinking of blood and bearing a servant of Nűműzóho on your back?" Pahninee pressed.

"I killed two of them today, two of the demons. And this woman is no evil spirit. She may not be flesh and blood

NO GUILT OF BLOODSHED

like you and I, but she's trying to beat back the darkness just the same as me. She was hurt, hurt worse than me, by one of the demons because she was helping me. We need a place to stay; we need a place to recover. She needs a place to be safe while I take care of the rest. You let us rest with you, and tomorrow I'll make for the barracks to kill your cannibal."

There was silence. Malechai scanned the faces, finally finding Pahninee's old face in the crowd. His mouth was a thin line, and there was no trust or allowance in his gaze. As Malechai watched, though, a woman lowered her rifle and jogged to his side to whisper something in his ear. His face softened and then crumpled in grief.

"You say she was hurt . . . the other demons, they . . . " Pahninee didn't want to put the crime into words, but Malechai knew what he was working so hard not to say.

"Yes." The word hung in the air for a long moment, and Malechai thought that even now, after everything, they would be turned away.

Then Pahninee shouted a few orders in his own language, the guns went down, and suddenly several women moved forward, helping Agrat off the horse, leading her away. Malechai growled as they tugged on Agrat and jumped off the horse to stop them. But as soon as his feet touched the ground, his ribs screamed and the world spun. A moment later, he had crashed into the ground, the twilight fading into darkness.

Malechai sat up with a gasp. He was in a tent, and it was dark. He looked down at himself and realized he was naked, covered with a thin sheet of linen and softer animal furs. He couldn't see much in the blackness of the tent, so he felt around for a moment, searching for his clothes and, more importantly, his gun. He was getting ready to rise from the bed to search for a weapon when the tent flap opened. He briefly caught sight of Agrat against the moonlight and back glow of the fires the Paiute burned before she stepped into the tent and closed the flap, plunging the interior into darkness again.

Mal felt Agrat sit next to him on the furs. He slowly lowered himself back down, staring up into the infinite darkness. "They didn't hurt you, did they?"

"I think the men wanted to, men only have two thoughts in their heads anyway, kill or fuck, usually both at the same time . . . " She said it blankly, with no accusation, as easily as one would say that the sky was blue or the night was black. "But women, women understand, and they helped tend to me as best a mortal can."

Mal nodded. "Good." He didn't argue with her; the first time they had enjoyed each other had been with his gun under her chin and her claws at his throat.

"You came for me, fought through hell. Why? Is your revenge against the priest really so pressing as to go through torture?"

"It is. He killed my brother, killed my people, and then came here and did the same." Mal sighed, letting his eyes close. "I'd follow that priest through any hell just to piss on his grave."

Agrat nodded in the darkness. Her knight in shining tallit had come not to rescue her but to fulfill his own needs. She shouldn't be surprised; this was the way of all men. But something sat wrong with the statement.

"Why didn't you take his deal, then? If all you're after is your priest, why didn't you just turn and walk away?"

Mal sat up, spilling the furs as he did. He searched for a moment and found her. He placed a hand on her thigh and felt her stiffen. He could feel her anger, the feelings of impotence her abuse had dredged up in her. "Wasn't going to do that, wasn't going to leave you to that kind of fate."

"Why not?" She brushed his hand aside. "You would have got what you want, and it would have cost you nothing."

"Because you deserve your freedom, you deserve to be

your own master." Malechai shrugged. "That's all any of us want, and that fat sack of shit is the antithesis of that. He represents everything my people have fled for thousands of years. Wasn't going to leave you in that situation, especially as it's my fault they came for you."

"He would have killed you."

"Yeah." He chuckled. "Almost did," Mal agreed as he lay back down. He turned his back to her, trying to find a comfortable position to lie in on the furs that made the bed.

"Look, Agrat, I'm not going to pretend that I always have the best intentions, won't even pretend I'm a good person. But I wasn't going to leave you in their hands, no matter what I needed, no matter if he had a seal or not, I would have come for you." He felt her shifting in the darkness, the rustling of fabric, and then she was slipping underneath the furs.

She pressed against his back, her softness intoxicating against his skin. She wrapped her arms around him but didn't say a word as they lay in the darkness together, each lost in their own thoughts, regrets, and painful memories.

Agrat didn't sleep. She didn't need to, technically, and her mind was aflame with too many thoughts, confusions, and rages to allow her peace. She listened to the scarred Jewish gunman snoring when he finally succumbed to slumber again. She rested her head against his back, her fingers—fingers that had torn angelic flesh hours ago—tracing slow intricate patterns on his chest as she considered all that had happened in the last couple of days and all that would be coming the next time the sun rose.

Malechai was like a force of nature. She was sure there was some supernatural blood in his past, some Sheydim or Malikim gift that pushed his endurance past all human expectations. But at the end of the day, she had tasted him, his sweat, his blood, his cum; he was a human man. But he was certainly a unique one. She watched him sleeping. He was not at peace; he twisted and turned, a cold sweat breaking out across his skin. His teeth ground in frustration at some unseen thing, and he yelped, panting in his sleep.

Agrat leaned forward, pressing her warm nakedness against him, and rested her forehead against his clammy skin. With a thought, she slipped into his dreams.

The battlefield was comparable to Sheol—gray mud marred with blood underfoot and made slick with rain and the fluids that kept men alive. Agrat, manifesting within the dream in a simple cotton dress, summoned a large coat and wrapped it around herself against the chill of the rain and wind in this desolate place. Everywhere she looked were the dead and dying. Men who had been torn apart by cannons. Some in gray and some in red, it was obvious that it had been a terrible battle. Men who had fought for something they may or may not even believe in were now ragged corpses and carrion, fit dining for the things that stalked after violence was done. Agrat passed by the bodies, ignoring the black birds that hung in the sky and the wolves that dragged the dead and almost dead away. There were men whose wounds were fresh laying on the bodies of men who had died a week ago on this unending battlefield. Agrat walked slowly and steadily through the tableau of blood, mud, and cruelty.

She found Malechai ben Palache on his knees at the center of the bloodbath. She could see it was him, recognize his black eyes and his dark hair. But his face was smooth— no scar tugging his face into its awful leer, no lines creased into the flesh by hard living and painful times. He looked up at her, surprised to see anything other than birds, wolves, and boars moving through the dead.

"Who goes there?" he asked in Russian, raising a bent and obviously broken rifle. Even his voice was young; he spoke with none of the gravel and hatred in his voice that had so colored the way Mal spoke now.

"I do," she responded, stepping out from behind the wreckage of a cannon. *"What is this place? Where are we?"*

"Crimea. Close to Balaclava . . . we were to take Balaclava, but . . . " He gestured to the carnage around him. *"They had so many . . . so many . . . "* He turned his head, hearing shouting further away on the battlefield. *"They sweep through now, making sure we are all dead . . . they'll find me soon, they'll find me, and they'll question me . . . "* He reached up and touched his cheek; when he pulled his hand away, that terrible scar was there.

"Is this, was this your first battle?" Agrat asked.

"Yes, it isn't how I thought it would be. I thought I would come home a hero. I would regale Ivanna and Yitzak with tales of bravery and victory, but they'll think I am dead." He hung his head, defeated.

"I cannot change the past, Malechai," Agrat whispered, stepping forward, placing a hand on his rifle, and gently pushing it down before she took his hand in hers. *"But that does not mean you have to relive it tonight."* She breathed in, and the world around them shimmered, the corpses and shouting faded, the scavengers all slinking away as a grand palace erected itself around them. Seemingly built of natural stone, the building shot up around them, encompassing them as the earth shook. Objects filled the palace, strange, magical, and decadent, and then a room formed around them. A bedroom made of the same stone but filled with pillows and soft things. But there were also suits of armor, weapons of war, art; this was the room of a noble and a warrior.

Malechai turned to face Agrat, and he was himself, with all the gristle, scars, and gravel that life had given him.

"What is this?" he asked.

"You were a cute kid, but I think I prefer the man," she answered, the flirtatious remark failing to hide the pain that swelled in both wounded creatures.

"I mean *this*, Agrat," he gestured at the room around them, "where are we?"

"We are in your dream, still . . . but this, this was home.

Before I was trapped in the box. Where I will return some day to see my family again." Agrat moved and sat on the bed, her dress and coat morphing into deep red wraps of silk. Likewise, Malechai's torn uniform became an unfathomably soft robe. "I thought maybe we deserved a comfortable place, or at least a break from the nightmares for a night."

Malechai nodded and moved to the armor. It was old, the sort the knights used to wear, stuff that had become worthless in an age of gunslingers. The swords next to the armor were beautiful, but from the nicks and scrapes along the blades, he could tell they weren't just for show.

"Malechai, what is your plan?" Agrat finally asked.

"Tomorrow morning, when it's still dark, I'll head to the barracks, set up a trap, hopefully, that will do enough damage and chaos that I can slip in and do what I need to without having to fight the entire American army stationed here. Get in, kill a demon, get out. You'll stay here, where it's safe . . . well, not here. With the Paiute, I mean."

Agrat rose from the bed and moved to stand beside him, wrapping her arm around his and pulling him back towards the bed. She gently pushed him onto the bed and shed her silks, standing in full, glorious nudity in front of him. Her hands traveled over her skin, caressing her curves. He shook his head and placed a hand flat on her stomach; the warmth of her skin was enough to drive him to distraction, but he focused.

"You don't need to do this, not for me."

She took his hand and moved it down between her legs, her fingers on his, guiding him to rub. "I told you before, I do who I wish; I am my own woman." She sighed gently, guiding his fingers inside of her. "In here, in this dream, I don't hurt, I'm not damaged or broken, and I want to be close." Her voice wavered. She lifted her hand, feeling him moving his fingers to massage her on his own, and reached down to cup his face. Her lips parted, and she sighed at the pleasure that spread through her body.

Mal continued to slide his fingers in and out of Agrat, his thumb massaging her clit as he reached with the other hand on her small waist to gently guide her onto the bed beside him. Agrat lay back, her body perfectly taut and writhing gently under his attention. He freed his hand and moved between her legs, planting kisses along her thigh, moving slowly up with each one. She watched him, raising an eyebrow, but then tossed her head back into the bed and arched her back as he found himself buried in her sex, licking, kissing, and gently sucking.

Three orgasms later, Agrat reached down and pulled Mal up to her, kissing him gently, unbothered by the sticky sweetness on his face and in his beard. She pushed the robes off of him, pulling him close. "I want you. I need you inside me, now," she whispered, nipping his ear before ducking her head to kiss and suck on his neck.

Malechai adjusted his position and submitted to her request.

Hours later, Malechai stared at the ceiling of Agrat's dream home. The ceiling was covered in tile, various shades of black creating subtle images and designs. It was beautiful, and Mal wondered if this was the sort of thing that was meant for human eyes. He slowly shifted, wincing at the sensitivity in his cock as it slid out of her.

She smiled and stretched cat-like before sitting up. His body reacted immediately to watching her move, and she smiled, reaching down to slowly stroke his stiffening meat. "In dreams, you don't have to worry about pesky things like stamina and the limits of your biology," she said, and then frowned slightly. "But it is getting late, and soon the sun will rise."

Malechai nodded gently, pulling himself from her grasp. "Then it's time I go."

CHAPTER TWELVE
... AND A TIME TO HATE; A TIME FOR WAR

MALECHAI EMERGED FROM the tent fully dressed. Agrat had helped clothe him in silence, something strangely intimate in the moment, as though the closeness they had experienced in his dreams was somehow more real, more meaningful than that first night they had spent together. When she had finished buttoning his shirt, she had looked up at him, hands on his chest. He knew that whatever this was, it was not permanent; she was using him. But even knowing that, he had leaned forward and kissed her, feeling her melt against him. Without a word, he had turned and left.

He was at his horse, checking the saddlebags, making sure nothing had been taken or touched, Mishpat was at his side, sitting patiently as if aware of the importance of today and the coming battle. Mal heard the elder, Pahninee, clear his throat from behind him.

"I'm heading to the garrison," Mal said without turning around to face the old man.

"So you said. There is a good chance you will die this morning." Pahninee's tone was almost conversational.

"Haven't been taken by Samael yet; don't plan on it being today," he responded before turning and looking at the old medicine man.

Pahninee stood there, staring up at the dark sky. The sun hadn't even started to lighten the horizon yet, which was good; he needed it dark. Pahninee sighed and held out a wad of white cloth, muslin by the look of it. Malechai took the fabric and uncrumpled it. It was a shirt.

"You asked for one of our magic shirts. This shirt has been made with Paiute magic, each thread woven with the blessings of the spirits to protect you from the white man's bullets."

Malechai nodded, looking over the shirt. Was it really magic? Why would he doubt it? He had just enjoyed a night of passion with a lover inside his mind, he had spoken to his dead brother in a makeshift hell created by an angel whose dick was in the saddlebag his hand now rested against. Was a shirt that could repel bullets any more strange? He considered too the coin with the Chinese god on it that had caught the bullet from Mammon's gun. Malechai quickly pulled off his coat, tallit, and overshirt so he could slip the muslin shirt on and redress.

"Thank you," he said to the old man.

"You're probably going to die, but now I can say that I did not send you to your death with no help. My conscience will be clean," Pahninee remarked.

"I suppose that's all that really matters then," Mal responded with a smirk as he pulled himself into the saddle.

"I'll be back for the woman," he promised, then kicked the horse gently in the ribs and headed off in the direction of Brodie.

The garrison was closer than the actual town, and for that, Malechai was pleased. It was still dark when he arrived, though the horizon was starting to look lighter. He needed it dark; his plan only worked if it was dark. Hitching the horse to a tree, Malechai made his final approach on foot, low to the ground, using what cover he could to stay out of sight. There were guards on watch, of course. Mal slipped through the shadows and positioned himself behind the men. One man was large, his huge gut hanging over his pants and stretching his uniform's buttons nearly to the breaking point. He smelled sour, like the moist shit and stale sweat he was unable to reach to wash away. The other man was not grotesque, but he shook. His head and limbs twitched and shivered despite the warm night air. Mal had seen the sort of symptom before, in desperate times, when the cold killed off the crops and there was no food to be had. Judging from the shaking, he wouldn't make it to the next season. Even without Malechai's intervention.

After a few moments of observation, he wrapped his arm around the shivering man's head, covering his mouth with his hand. He jerked the man's chin up and cut through the skin, jugular, and vocal cords in one swift motion, nearly tearing through to the spine from ear to ear. Without pausing, he stepped back. The fat man turned at the sound of his friend's body falling, but before he could even ask what was wrong, Malechai materialized from the shadows and jammed the knife through the man's eye, cutting through the jelly and into the brain until the crossbar of the knife crunched into the bone of the man's eye socket. Mal used his shoulder to push the massive man back and watched him spasm and die in the dirt.

Quickly, Mal looked around and made sure there were no other patrols coming and then set to work. He worked quickly and efficiently, moving the dead bodies and setting up the surprise he had in store for the men inside the barracks. After he was done, Malechai retreated a good distance from the fort, hid behind a tree, and lifted the Shofar to his lips. He gave it a mighty blow and then fired his gun at the fort several times. Ducking back behind the tree, Malechai reloaded as he listened to the sounds of panic as the fort slowly stirred to wakefulness.

Moments later, he heard the shouts as emerging soldiers tripped over the dead Malechai had left in front of the doors to the base. In moments, they would light the lanterns to search out the surroundings. Mal took a deep breath, rolling his shoulders and finding his center.

The explosion that followed as the soldiers lit lanterns where Mal had replaced the candles and wicks with sticks of dynamite was almost deafening. But it was nothing compared to the next few explosions that were triggered from that first boom. Body parts rained from the sky as screams and shouts filled the dawn. The sun was coming up, revealing a bloody dust filled air that now hung over the fort.

It also revealed an army of Paiute watching just a bit away. Mal held his breath, surprised to see the natives, but as they kicked their horses and began riding into battle, all thoughts and reason left. Mal abandoned his position behind the tree and joined the charge against the swiftly organizing army base.

Bullets whizzed past in each direction as the soldiers poured out of the base like ants. They organized too quickly; they were too well prepared for an attack. His opening ambush and trap should have thrown the entire base into disarray. It was with grim understanding that Malechai came to the realization that the demon inside had prepared them for his coming. It was a cold knowledge that if the Paiute hadn't shown up and joined this battle, he would be dead no matter how clever he was.

Malechai fired his revolver into the oncoming flood of white men in khaki wool uniforms. A man died gurgling blood as he collapsed, only to be trampled into the dirt by his compatriots as they charged. Malechai fired again, bursting the left eye of another soldier. He kept firing. Five more times the hammer fell, five more of the flood fell. Malechai growled, pushing the gun into his belt and drawing his sword. It was a bloodbath as men of every color were put to ground with holes ripped through their fresh corpses. There was nothing romantic or poignant about the battle; there never was. Mal had killed his way across dozens of war zones and front lines. The one constant was that there was chaos. He jumped over a dying man and flung himself into the thick of it, spinning the blade in his hand as he sliced through one man's throat only to turn the blade in his hand to disembowel another.

Mal ducked under a bayonet thrust and headbutted the man coming towards him. Reaching forward, he pulled the man's sidearm out of his belt and fired it into his gut before turning to find a new target. He was suddenly thrown back as the force of a musket ball slammed into his chest, bowling him backwards and over a corpse. Mal checked his chest; his ribs hurt, but there was no blood. The shirt had stopped the projectile.

"I'll be fucked sideways." He growled as he rose from the ground.

The native Paiute had a huge advantage over the more numerous soldiers. But was it enough? They weren't invincible, and with a quick glance around, Malechai saw that those Paiute who had taken a bullet to the head or a blade to the chest were still joining the dead and dying. The shirts gave them an edge against the soldiers, but it didn't make any of this clear cut or easy. Malechai jumped backwards out of the way of a brutal bayonet stab before springing forward and ramming his sword down the man's throat and out through the spinal column on the other side. Malechai slashed through another man as he rushed forward, severing his hand before bringing the stolen revolver around and emptying the four remaining bullets into onrushing men. He pressed forward. He killed as he moved, grabbing a dead man's gun whenever he ran out of ammo, cutting those who got close enough to use his sword against. He carved a bloody swathe through the battlefield, unrelenting and unmerciful. Even if he had to abandon the Paiute to this battle, he had to get inside the fort and come face to face with the final demon.

Malechai slipped between the ruined gates of the fort. The TNT he had set his trap with had destroyed the doors and much of the stonework. But the soldiers were too focused on the Paiute threat ahead of them to turn back and notice the intruder. Out there with the fighting, it was a bloodbath, but inside the fort, it was a charnel house. Rotting bodies lay everywhere he looked, they had been gnawed on or cut into pieces. They were all cannibals.

Corpses of every shape and size, in various stages of decay, hung from meat hooks that dangled over doors and from every available ledge. Malechai took a step forward, wincing as the ground squelched underfoot, made into a brackish mud from the shear amount of blood and putrefying offal that saturated the earth. Above the fort, hundreds of vultures circled, nearly invisible in the early morning sky. The birds of death resembled a cyclone of carrion feeders. And they were centered above one building.

Malechai tossed aside the pistol he had taken off a dead man and pulled his own gun from his belt. He reloaded as he walked towards what must be the mess hall. With every step, his boots sunk into the ground, and he could not avoid stepping on half devoured carcasses. The fort looked like the den of some rabid beast more than any sort of organized group. He had expected most of the corpses to be natives, but saw Chinese, Mexican, and many white men and women in the piles of meat stacked against buildings. He paused when his foot crunched down and looked to see a small child-sized ribcage stuck on his boot. He kicked it off with a growl. The smell was painful, the acrid scent of rot so thick in the air it stung his eyes.

Malechai threw open the doors to the mess hall and almost fell back; the foul stench of rot and carnage was overpowering in the small building. Bodies were piled everywhere, all the way to the ceiling. The rot and liquefying organs sloshed under his feet as he stepped into the hot building, squinting into the darkness. Where there were no bodies, there were spider webs. Things with far too many legs and eyes skittered in the shadows of the unlit room. Malechai took another step, swinging the revolver between one shadow and the next. Was it possible the demon had actually joined the battle outside? Was it ripping apart the Paiute as he wasted his time jumping at shadows?

Something brushed his back, and he whirled, bringing the gun around. She was there, a tall, emaciated woman in a gore-soaked white slip. She looked like skin had been tortuously stretched over a frame too small for it and then been given some semblance of life. Her dry, cracked lips turned up in a smile as empty eye sockets that seemed to contain eternity swallowed what little light was seeping through the open door. Behind her spread twenty-six chitinous legs, thirteen pairs of arachnid limbs sprouting from her back that whipped forward, entangling him, spinning him, and lifting him off the ground. His gun fell to the floor as he was jerked up into the rafters and the darkness. He felt the strands of webbing enveloping him, holding him tight as the knife edges of the demon's legs scraped against him and turned him.

"Hello, little killer." The voice was paper thin and scraped against his mind.

Malechai struggled against the webbing, but it was like being wrapped in iron chains. Spindly fingers coated black with ash flittered across his face before gripping either side of his head painfully and forcing him to look into the demon's empty sockets. Her lips were so thin that her mouth appeared like a crack in dry rotted wood, it opened in an "o" of surprise, the stretching skin painful to even look at, but she would not let him turn his face away from her.

"Oh, I like you, I . . . " She tusked her head in close, inhaling deeply as she breathed in his scent. "You have the hatred in you, you have my gift . . . " She sniffed him again, then leaned back, staring at him in amusement. "Oh . . .

little niece, little niece, come out, come out and tell me why you've sent this man to die." Tanin'iver released Malechai, and he swung in the webbing that suspended him from the ceiling. From the shadows near the door, he watched Agrat step forward.

"Hello, Aunt Tani," Agrat whispered, and it floated above the sounds of battle outside, barely audible. Agrat looked down, unwilling to meet Malechai's eyes.

"Mm, free quite some time and this is the first you've visited. Visiting in the shadow of a killer who comes for my head." Tanin'iver's head jerked towards Mal. "Don't be surprised I can smell the murderous intention on you. I can taste your blood lust, your . . . kavanah." She reached back and tore a strip of putrid meat from a nearby corpse and pushed it towards Mal, who closed his lips tight. She used her other hand to grip his chin and pull, forcing her fingers between his teeth. "Eat, or the next strip I offer will be from your own body," she hissed.

Mal relented to her force as she shoved the rancid, sour meat between his lips. He chewed, nearly gagging on the taste. The too familiar flavor of human flesh filled his mouth and coated his tongue with the slime of decay. He choked as he forced the meat down.

"So, answer, little niece, answer me." Tanin'iver turned her eyeless gaze back down to Agrat and skittered around Malechai, poking and prodding, like an insect that could not sit still for want of a meal. "You sent him here. You knew he would fail, that he would die. Or . . . or you thought he wouldn't, and you wanted me dead. So which is it? Which of us did you hope to see choking on blood this morning? Why do the soldiers who follow me and the natives of this land kill each other outside? They die only so this man could come into my home and die by my hands. But why did you will this into being?"

"Aunt Tanin'iver—"

"Ah, full names," the demoness interrupted. "Now you are being serious, good."

"I neither wanted you nor Malechai dead. You can taste his hostility towards the purists; you said he has the same hatred as you. You are kindred spirits. Beliya'al thought he had the mark of Azazel, but I don't believe that. I believe he is yours."

"Mine?" the Sheyd spat. "I do not claim the souls of the simple creatures as the Watchers do. What use have I for such things? And no . . . " Tanin'iver came forward, licking Mal's face with a long black tongue that dripped ichor and left a trail of burning sludge on his face. "I taste the warmonger. Tell me why he is here, and do not lie again, Agrat bat Lillit."

"I am here to kill you," Malechai roared, spitting the last bits of rotting flesh out. "To kill you and break the seals protecting the church. I'm going to kill you so I can raise my pistol and shoot that dog priest down, right under his fucking cross."

"At least one of you is honest." Tanin'iver drew back her terrible clawed hand, ready to tear his throat out.

"Wait!" Agrat screamed, and then softer, "Wait, I brought him here because of the war, Aunt Tani. he fights without knowing, he fights because it's in his heart and his will. Taste his thoughts and you'll know he's as much a warrior of the War of Dictates as any mortal can be," Agrat panted, pleading with her terrible aunt.

Tanin'iver sneered at her niece but relented, using the insect legs of her back to gather Malechai in close. "So she says, so she believes." The withered Sheyd grabbed his face once more and put her forehead against his.

His world plunged into darkness, a deep muddy pit of pain and despair where lost souls were denied the light of God. The cold saturated the damp air, which in turn seeped into his bones, stealing away all resolve and willpower. In that dark muddy place, he saw the countless dead, the same dead he had seen on the path to the jail. Those he had killed in wars, battles, and brawls. Each man or woman was chained by a rusted manacle around the neck in an alcove of running mud that stank the stench of unclean intestines left in the sun. Among the hundreds of dead he had sent beyond Gehenna, to Tzoah Rotachat, amongst all the dead he had sent to this dread place, he saw an empty alcove, and he knew, knew in his freezing, brittle bones, that it was meant for him.

Chains capped with meat hooks shot from the darkness of the empty alcove, whipping wildly, tearing through his flesh, hooking into his very soul, and pulling him forward towards his new torturous home. Mal growled in pain, hiding his despair behind defiance. He struggled against the chains, digging in his heels, trying to fight them, to grab his gun, his sword, anything that he could fight the chains with. But it was as hopeless as fighting time—a relentless killer that all efforts fell flat against. He roared his rage out, unwilling to be dragged into the grave without a fight.

"I . . . " Tanin'iver stuttered, pulling back from Malechai.

The muddy depths of Tzoah Rotachat faded. There were no chains, just the hellish tableau of half-eaten corpses in the mess hall. Mal swung from the ceiling, powerless, tears running down his face; he could still feel the meat hooks in his flesh, the cold of Gehenna frosted his breath even outside of the vision.

"The priest you hunt, I saw his deeds, I see his fear and his will to wipe your kind out. We have seen through each other's eyes now, Malechai ben Palache." She hung there, suspended from the ceiling in silence by her arachnid legs.

"Aunt Tani, I told you, kindred spirits," Agrat said softly.

"You also know what you are asking me; you know what it will cost me . . . imprisonment, again," Tanin'iver stated.

"I know," Agrat said, somewhat sadly.

Tanin'iver moved suddenly, gripping Malechai's chin, forcing his ugly, scarred face to look into her deep empty sockets. "Listen to me, mortal, I set my oath on you, a curse. If and when you see the downtrodden, should you do nothing, I will come for you. No seal, no ward, no holy place can keep me from you. You are an avenger now, and the priest will be but the first you put in the ground. This is the price I set on you; this is the curse I set before you. Swear it and live in pain and rage, or refuse and die in peace."

"I swear," Malechai growled. This wasn't something he needed to think about; this wasn't a question he had to debate. He had given up peace before he realized he was making a choice. His life had been nothing but bloodshed and violence, and if continuing that life meant that he got to murder the ungodly priest and avenge his brother, it was really nothing he needed to think about.

Tanin'iver nodded and released him, one bladed limb coming up over her head to strike forward and sever the threads that held Malechai there. He tumbled to the ground, his fall broken by corpses. Agrat hurried forward and pulled him up, helping him find his footing. He looked up for the terrible demoness, but she was already gone. They were alone.

Mal turned on Agrat, pulling his arm free. "Your fucking aunt? You didn't think maybe that would be some information worth sharing with me?" His hand hovered over his empty holster. He looked around the corpse-strewn floor and found his weapons. He sheathed the sword, the gun he still held in a hand that shook from anger.

"I came, didn't I? I came to make sure she didn't hurt you," Agrat responded, defending herself, though she already sounded defeated.

"You didn't poke your head out until she told you to. Lucky for me, she was in a talking mood. What would you have done if she just started eating me? You could have just waltzed in here with me, told me your plan."

"I didn't have a plan, Malechai."

"Don't fucking lie to me, girl!" he roared back at her. "I

may not be much to look at, I may not be the most educated or cleverest man in the world, but goddamnit, I am not an idiot. I know when I'm being manipulated. I know when I'm being used."

Agrat's face hardened. "If you think I'm just using you, you're a moron and an idiot, but you believe what the fuck you want to believe." She held his gaze in defiance. It was the same raging power she had shown their first night together. The will of solid steel that revealed itself when he accused her of just using him for food.

They held there, both too set on edge by the harrowing encounter with Tanin'iver to breathe easy and both too proud to look away first. After several minutes, it was Malechai who broke the stare.

He holstered his revolver and shook his head. When he spoke, he sounded tired, too exhausted to fight with her on top of the rest of the world. "Get out of here, Agrat. Just . . . go to town, wait for me there, near the church."

"What are you going to do?" she asked, the edge still in her voice, a blade that needed to cut someone down.

"I'm going to finish up here, and then I'm going to go kill the priest, but I think I would like it if you weren't with me while I ride back." He fixed her with a look.

She met it with anger, frustration, and sadness warring in her eyes before wordlessly turning and marching out of the charnel mess hall.

Malechai emerged from the fort and walked the battlefield. Around him, the Paiute were gathering their dead, scavenging what weapons and material they could. Mal was also scavenging; knife in hand, he knelt in the blood drenched mud and pulled one of the dead soldiers' pants down and sawed through the discolored and scabbed flesh of his cock.

"Winnemucca! What are you doing?!" Pahninee's voice was full of revulsion and terror. The old man had wanted peace, and now, he was not only party to terrible bloodshed but was witnessing this man he had helped desecrating the dead and disrespecting their bodies.

Mal paused, resting his knife hand on his knee as he reached down with his left hand, gripped the flaccid meat, and ripped, tearing the flesh and meat away from the body before tossing it in his burlap sack. "Collecting payment," he answered.

"No, this is . . . this is evil, what you are doing. They have already paid the price, they are dead. Leave them be," Pahninee said, his voice raising in anger and challenge.

"Leave them be," Mal repeated as he stood up, adjusting the grip on his knife. Around him, the natives were slowly raising their rifles, taking aim, amped up on battle lust, keenly aware of the great threat the man in the tallit represented. "Leave them be? While I sailed from my country to yours, do you know what the main conversation was? It was how much coin a man could get for a scalp. An Indian scalp." He spread his arms wide, and the natives took steps back from the blood drenched Jew.

"How much coin they could get for murdering your people, and how they could maybe kill light skinned Africans and Mexicans and pass them off." He turned in a tight circle, meeting the eyes of those holding the weapons. "They laughed as they talked about size! They asked if a child's scalp would go for as much as a full-grown man's! Or if they should sew together multiple children's flesh so they could get more cash for the effort. They spoke on if they should rape the women before or after the scalping, which was more fun, more pleasureful."

The guns that had been aimed at Mal slowly fell away as the natives listened and relived their own memories of lost loved ones.

"Leave them be?" he repeated before continuing his rant. "And these men, these men are flesh eaters. These are the monsters from your stories. Look inside their fort and see the kindness they visited on the dead. Look inside and tell me that a single one of these men deserves rest of kindness; tell me that they paid the price for their deeds in death! Tell me that they earned that peace."

Mal dropped his arms. "Leave them be." His voice was full of venom and rage. "The only kindness these so-called men get from me is that they're dead before I work, Pahninee. I ain't stopping. Now you can shoot me dead, though I suspect you won't like what happens next." A deep growl that originated from somewhere not of this earth echoed from the clay jaws of Mishpat as it came up from behind the Elder. Malechai ignored it, and Pahninee, as he moved to another body and knelt in the thick soup of viscera and dirt to cut away the dead man's pants.

This time, no one interrupted his grisly task.

CHAPTER THIRTEEN
BY DEEDS, NOT BY WORDS

AS HE MOUNTED his horse and turned back towards Brodie, Malechai was struck by the violence he had wrought in just three days. He was no good man; he was no kind soul. He had rolled into town with hatred hardening his heart like the story of Pharaoh in the Exodus. But whereas the men in that story dealt with supernatural plagues, he had come into town as a plague himself. He rode, Mishpat trotting next to him, not hurrying. His body and soul ached, and for some reason he didn't understand, his heart felt heavy.

His body hurting was no mystery. Over the last three days, he had fought near constantly. He had taken the boot of a demon to the chest and taken enough hits to take a lesser man out to a shallow grave. The supernaturally good luck he had had by not being shot down or gutted yet was not lost on him. But he was far from invincible; the scars he wore on his skin were testament to his all too real mortality. He took a few minutes to take a mental inventory of his body. Nothing was clicking or refusing to bend, and so long as his body obeyed him, he could take the fury and vengeance of his rage down on Risti's head. He had been hurt before, more times than he could count; he would never let something so simple as being beaten like a dog by an angel stand in the way between him and revenge.

His soul aching was a surprise, but again, there was no question as to the reason. A man could steep himself in bloodshed his whole life and not feel a thing, but as it became personal, it wore on the spiritual body. Mal was sure that it was mentioned somewhere in the Torah, but he would be damned if he could think of the verse that spoke on revenge. Probably wasn't too favorable. But favorable or not, this was what he was good at; it was all he was good at. He would chase that bloody end so long as his boots met earth.

He thought back to the oath that the demon Tanin'iver had set before him. A curse he had immediately agreed to taking on: an avenger, defender of the downtrodden. He considered the words she had used, the power behind them. At the time, it had seemed very straightforward. She would kill him if he didn't agree, and she hadn't been asking anything so painful or costly that he wouldn't have agreed, anyway. But she had promised that Risti was just the first, and that he would live as an avenger. That in taking her deal, he would live in rage and blood. In truth, it wasn't what he had wanted. His life had been one wallowed in so much bloodshed that he could never wash the stains of his deeds from his skin, but he had wanted to. He had decided to settle in that little frontier town with his siblings; he had decided to look for a wife, to retire the sword and pistol in exchange for a plowshare and a quiet life.

Risti had taken that from him. Blood had followed him into the town on the lips of a Christian demagogue. The women he had courted, the friends he had made, his brother . . . all dead. Dead by a mob that followed the words of a manipulator above that of their supposed god. There was nothing else he could do but delve into the world he had been presented.

What about his heart? Why did that ache? Malechai lifted a hand and touched his chest. He wasn't well versed in dealing with emotional pain. And he had been forced to face his dead brother, confronting his grief and—possibly more importantly—his guilt over his brother's death. He thought about the nightmarish landscape that the fallen angel Beliya'al had forced him to traverse, which reminded him of the reason he had decided he would rather take on the full might of an angel than take the easy route. It wasn't that much of a shock; Malechai had never been one to take the easy route in life. The ride after had been harder than the fight; his body had been pushed beyond human endurance already, and riding all the way to the Paiute with Agrat had been nearly impossible.

Malechai's scarred face pulled down into a dour frown. That night in his dreams had been different than other nights with other women. It had been in a dream, a strange world in and of itself, but she had brought him within that dream, to her home, not just her bed but the place she longed for. There was something more intimate about sharing your safest place with another. He had sent her away, to wait for him at the church. But he had felt like she betrayed his trust, left him to hang in Tanin'iver's horrible webs.

But still, the thought that by sending her ahead of him he wasn't keeping her close to protect against whatever else the demons could throw at him set ill within his chest. It made his stomach flip. More manipulation, he told himself. She was a succubus, a demonic lillikim whose entire purpose was the manipulation of men's emotions and lust. He wouldn't be stupid enough to fall into her trap. But that would mean ignoring his heart and ignoring that she had brought him out of his nightmares and to her home. That she had followed him into a hellish battlefield, risking cannibals and demons to confront her terrifying aunt. Her aunt whom he had sworn an oath to. He was embroiled in the affairs of demons and angels now, likely no extricating himself. And if he were to live a life embroiled in their bullshit, least he could do was find some warmth and enjoyment in that. Something . . . good.

Malechai had just resolved himself to make good with Agrat when he noticed that the streets of Brodie were emptier than usual. When he had first come to town, the place was bustling and wicked. With hundreds dead from the violence he had brought with him in just a few days, perhaps now the inhabitants of the town were thinking better of poking their heads out. All the better.

The sun was overhead, baking the earth beneath him, surrounding him in a stifling heat. Mal turned down the main street towards St. Cyprian's church and saw the lone man standing in the center of the road.

The man was a tall, gaunt ghost of a man, long and lean, dressed entirely in black save for the stark white of a preacher's collar and the flash of silver from a colt revolver on his belt. Malechai dismounted and patted the horse on the side, leading it to the edge of the road. He didn't know who the man was, or if it were actually a man, but he recognized the challenge. "Stay here," Mal told the mastiff shaped golem and walked back to the middle of the road, approaching the other man.

"This isn't your fight, priest," Malechai called when he was far enough that he wouldn't have to strain his voice.

"The fight against evil is always my fight. That is my cross to bear, but I am no priest," the man responded, his voice like the deep rumblings of canyons during an avalanche of stone.

Malechai stopped a dozen paces from the man. "You dress like the servants of the Christian's god. Haven't seen one carrying a pistol before now, but you look like a priest."

"Not all men of God are priests and Catholics. I am a reverend, a man of God, though not the kind, gentle God of the New Testament but rather the—"

"Kind and gentle? You haven't been paying attention." Malechai snarled, "You Christians are death dealers and defilers, only serving the light to climb into the shadows above you."

The reverend's ice-blue eyes narrowed. "You may lay

your accusations at my feet, but you are damned by deeds, and I will be God's judgment on this earth, even as Satan presides over your soul in hell."

Mal didn't need to listen to more proselytizing from another hypocrite that carried a book in one hand and a hangman's noose in the other. In one smooth motion, he drew and fired. The reverend was faster, so fast it seemed like the colt had leapt from his belt to his hand and fired. Both men wheeled back, touched by the wind of the passing bullets as they scrambled for cover. Mal dove behind a small stack of water barrels in front of the general store where he had bought his knife. He hadn't seen where the reverend had got to. He poked his head just above the barrels and was rewarded by wood splinters to the face as the reverend's shot dug in inches from him.

"You are a good shot, Christian!" Malechai called over the distance. "You didn't always wear that collar; you were a soldier, weren't you?" Malechai ducked low and peeked around the other side of the barrels. He saw the preacher's shadow poking from behind a building's corner. He fired, clipping the edge of the building and sending the shadow dancing back.

"I believe it takes one to know one, but do not think that old camaraderie will do you favors or lead me to any leniency in carrying out my holy duty." With uncanny accuracy, the preacher stepped out of cover and fired. One bullet slammed into the barrels where Mal had been, the other cut through the shoulder of his coat. The man had corrected his aim in a hair's breadth.

Mal returned a shot, but it went wide as he scrambled back into cover. "I doubt we fought in any war on the same side. What is your name?" Mal called. Despite himself, there was some joy in this. This was the first real challenge he had faced in Brodie. Other men had fallen easily to his blade and his gun. The demons had hurt him, but they weren't a fair match. But this, one man against one man, there was a purity in the moment.

NO GUILT OF BLOODSHED

"I am Reverend Jedidiah Mercer, and it is my curse from God to hunt evil, evil like you, Covington. I've been hunting you since Texas, across the Chisholm Trail and the Rockies. Now I have you, I will not let your evil continue, rest assured of that." Another bullet bit into the ground where Malechai had been.

Mal popped up and fired quickly, sending three shots towards the reverend. He had no idea who this fool thought he was, but he would be damned if a case of mistaken identity ended up being the end of his life. Ducking back down, he glanced back towards his horse and Mishpat. The golem was waiting exactly where he had told him to stay, unable to go against the command, or maybe not bright enough to. He whistled low, gesturing for the creature to circle around and flank the reverend. Mishpat started to move. Mal stood and sent another shot towards the reverend to keep him occupied while the Golem got in position.

The reverend returned the fire, and a bullet went through the top of Mal's hat, blowing it off his head. Mal glanced back at the bowler as it tumbled across the ground, then turned back and smiled as he saw the shadow of a hound approaching the shadow of the preacher.

"Not today, demon!" the reverend shouted, and there was a blaze of light from the alley the reverend was hiding in.

Mal didn't spare a second to consider what that might be; he was already vaulting over the barrels and racing towards the distracted preacher. Malechai slid around the corner and found the reverend surrounded by a circle of bible pages that had been ripped out and now burned with a strange fire without being consumed. Jedidiah's attention was on the clay mastiff that had rebounded off his strange barrier and was stalking just outside of his circle still smoldering. Malechai ignored the barrier, stepping over the fiery word of the Christian god to press his revolver against the back of the preacher's head.

"Goodbye, Reverend." Malechai pulled the trigger.

The revolver's hammer came down on the empty chamber with a resounding click. In the excitement of the shootout, Mal had not counted his shots, and now he was empty. He reached down to draw his blade, but Jedidiah was once again faster, whirling in place and shooting. Mal tumbled backwards at the force of the impact. The magic of the shirt held up, but the force of the point-blank shot had certainly cracked a rib and sent him sprawling. He landed on his back and pushed off the ground to try to rise when he saw Jedidiah's pistol pointed at his face. He stopped, his lips curling back in a snarl made all the uglier from the scar across his face.

"Your wicked days finally come to an end, Salem, no more black magic and murder, no more deal with Satan. Today, the Black Magpie dies."

"I don't know who you think I am, Reverend, but my name is neither Salem nor Covington. My name is Malechai ben Palache," Mal growled up at his doom.

Jedidiah paused, though his aim did not waver. "You are claiming you are not Salem Covington . . . " His blue eyes darted back to the dog, then back to Mal before Mal could even consider using the distraction to move. "I admit there are . . . inconstancies," he finally said. "Covington travels with a stagecoach, and I had not heard of him traveling with a hell hound. Then again, your scar speaks volumes. How many dark gunmen with scarred faces travel through the frontier?"

"And is your Salem Covington a Jew?" Mal spat.

The Reverend seemed to consider the tallit and kippah for a moment. "No, certainly not." He raised the barrel of his pistol until it was between Mal's eyes. "But even still, your hell hound proves your nature. Even if you are not Salem Covington, you are an evil man."

"It's not a fucking hell hound, it is a golem, a creature made of clay and empowered by HaShem. It was made to help me hunt demons," Mal said as quickly as he could get the words from between his lips.

"HaShem?"

"HaShem! Adonai, Elohai, God, whatever you call the God of Jews." Mal growled, exasperated.

"And you hunt demons?" The reverend sounded unconvinced.

"This town is saturated with demonic filth, led by one evil man, a man who pretends to be a man of god, a priest. I've been here three days, and I've hunted down five of their leaders. I was on my way to finish this when you stopped me." Mal's eyes stayed on the barrel of the gun, but so long as the reverend was talking, he wasn't shooting.

"A priest? A priest told me you were coming this way." His eyes darted towards the three-armed cross on top of the Greek Orthodox church at the center of town.

"That would be the one." Malechai's eyes noticed that behind the preacher, his bible pages were beginning to sputter out. Soon Mishpat would be able to get to him.

"In truth, he did seem off. He did not sit well with me." After another moment, the reverend pushed his pistol into the sash at his waist and offered Malechai his hand.

"It seems I owe you an apology. Though we are not brothers of the cloth, we serve the same God and the same mission." Malechai took the offered hand and allowed the surprisingly robust older man to pull him up. "It is only right that I help you take down this servant of Lucifer."

Mal shook his head. While help might be appreciated, he had already figured the reverend for a zealot. Should he join him, the reverend would likely take issue with Malechai having made a deal with one of the demons, and even if he turned a blind eye to that, would try to kill Agrat along with Risti. "No, this is something I must do alone. I've hunted the priest from the old world. It is . . . my burden to spill his blood. You should continue your quest for this Magpie."

Mishpat padded past the ashes of the bible pages and the preacher to sit by Malechai's feet.

The reverend stroked his chin, considering this Jew

and his golem. There was evil here, but he understood personal missions. He understood that each man who was called to be an avenger against the forces of evil had to follow their own path through this world, cutting a path of righteousness through the haze of the wicked. Finally, he nodded. "I have spent enough time here, and Covington does already have the lead. Very well, Malechai, may the lord guide your revolver, and may he remind you to reload." The corner of Mercer's mouth turned up in the slightest hint of humor as he raised his hand.

Malechai took the hand and shook it before turning away from the preacher to fetch his horse. When he turned back around, Mercer was gone. Malechai considered the man and said a silent prayer on behalf of Salem Covington, whoever he was. Jedidiah did not seem to be a man who gave up.

He continued back to his horse, Mishpat padding beside him. There was only one more thing to do, one more life to take. He took the horse by the reins, not bothering to mount back up, and walked with the beast in hand towards the church. Mal had to smile—as best as he was able through the pain and the scar tissue—as he thought about how desperate and terrified Risti must be. The Greek was enlisting mortal mercenaries now. But Mal had put men, demons, and even a goddamned angel in the ground. He wasn't about to stop. Not until every drop of sin and pain had been wrung from the priest's corpse.

Malechai stopped outside the doors of the church and looked around for a moment. Remembering Jedidiah's parting shot, he took the time now to reload his revolver. No sign of Agrat. Perhaps his anger at the garrison had driven her off completely; maybe abandoning him had always been her plan. Even knowing she was a creature of manipulation and deceits, his chest felt heavy. The logical mind and the heart had precious little to do with one another. He shook off the feeling; he hadn't come to America to find love; he hadn't traveled across the world to Brodie for a warm bed. He had come to murder a priest; that was still very much on the table. Malechai grabbed the saddlebags off the horse. One side had all the things he had collected through his killing spree: the dented coin with the Chinese war god, balm, the stacks of charms, the shofar, TNT, and the gold he had taken from the bank wagon. All the tools that had made his blood-drenched quest possible. The other side was filled with the bounty he had cut from Brodie's men. Agrat may have abandoned him, but he was a man of his word. He hefted the bags onto his shoulders; they were heavy with the weight of wasted and rotting potential.

"Come," Malechai commanded the golem as he pushed through the doors of the damned church.

CHAPTER FOURTEEN
NO GUILT OF BLOODSHED

THE CHURCH WAS shrouded in shadows. Throughout the building, gas lamps with red glass bathed the entire interior with a blood red light that barely pierced the shadows. Within the shadows, dark shapes writhed and beckoned. Demons with no bodies, spirits of malice and wanton self-denigration, whispered hate-filled promises. They offered lust and violence in equal measure. Mal pulled his tallit close around his shoulders and whispered a psalm of protection in Hebrew under his breath. It was said that if one was able to perceive all the demons in the world, that person would surely die. The sheer weight of negative emotion and animosity within the church made Mal believe it.

Just inside the doors to the church, on each side of the door, was a woman. Each was naked but for straps of steel that dug into her body and held her body stiff. The women were forced to their knees by the restraints. Their mouths had been pried open and held agape by leather straps. Dried semen coated lips and chins, several teeth had been forcefully removed to ensure a smooth fit. The women's lidless eyes were forced straight ahead, weeping clotted, bloody tears. They were the welcome mats, a taste of the pleasures you could enjoy or the tortures you could endure under the ministrations of the ministry ensconced within. Malechai looked between the women who writhed in fear

NO GUILT OF BLOODSHED

and pain, standing between them, considering them. They had done no wrong to him. But were they willing participants in the degeneracy of this unholy place? Were they woman who had come to this place seeking these twisted pleasures? Or were they victims? Stolen off the streets like the Chinese children had been?

Mal shook his head and drew his gun. The woman on his right leaned forward, moaning wordless platitudes. As he brought the gun up, she pressed her head against the barrel, no clearer sign than that. These women could not be saved; their minds and bodies were savaged. Only the holy one, blessed be, could salve their souls and flense the pain from their beings. The retort of the gunshots echoed throughout the church as he released one woman and then the other. He steeled himself and flicked open his revolver, reloading immediately, before he took several steps into the church.

Just a few feet into the church and he had already seen enough. Even if Mal had not been here to end the priest for his sins against the Jews of Odessa, the treatment of the victims would have convinced him to kill the man. Mal was no pure thing. He had sat in the torturer's chair as both victim and master more times than he could count. But he had never done so for fun, never for the sake of delivering pain upon those who had less power. That was the sign of a weak man.

Further in, Mal found more women and men who had been pinned to walls or hung from chains, dripping blood and drool from skinless faces and mouths with no lips, those who had sought absolution but been found wanting. They all lived, if one could call it that. These bleeding tortured things, their bellies had been cut open and their intestines draped across the church like garland or a bloody shit-filled spiderweb stretched between the bodies that groaned from the rafters. Malechai stepped between the drippings of bodies as he made his way to the front of the church.

There he stood, Dragan Risti, the butcher of Odessa, the priestly progenitor of pogroms who had directed the maddened masses of the Ukraine against the Jews. He was dressed in the black dour robes of the Greek Orthodoxy, the red trim and lining of the robes indistinguishable from the blood red light filling the chamber. Despite the low light, the gold chains and rings he wore glittered. He smiled, his dirty white beard parting to reveal thin lips and teeth that had been filed to points. He lifted one hand in a benediction, making the sign of the cross towards Malechai. His other hand held a gaudy and ostentatious knife to Agrat's throat. She was on her knees at his feet. She shot the priest a hateful glare before looking at Malechai. Her face softened. She looked ashamed for being caught.

"You keep getting caught by my enemies, going to start taking it the wrong way, Agrat."

"Her betrayal was no surprise, Jew, no surprise at all. It isn't the first time she tried to enlist some hapless fool in her mission, forgetting that it was I who freed her." Dragan spoke with the slur of the intoxicated.

"I'm not special then?" Mal asked with feigned disappointment.

"No, when you came to town you were likely the only man in Brodie she had not taken to bed," Dragan replied with a deranged grin.

What was it with weak-willed men like him? They always assumed that everyone shared their hoarding, needy possessiveness. How could a creature like him, who kept women chained as public receptacles for the ejaculate of all, care even the slightest about perceived purity?

"Well, shit, how many of the other men she laid with put your demons in the dirt?" He approached the altar, his eyes on the priest but attention on the blade he held at Agrat's throat. "How many of them dismantled your army and broke your seals and stood before you? Because, to be honest with you, priest, after chasing you all the way from Odessa, I am feeling rather special."

The priest's arm moved, pressing the blade to Agrat's throat, and Mal froze. "From Odessa, you're one of them? You came for the box." The priest threw his head back and laughed. "You can't possibly understand the power I have, Jew. You may have defeated my generals, my seals, but so long as I have the box, I have its power, I have the strength of every demon that remains free, I have their gifts. A deal made for their freedom. You will not get the box back, Jew; you will not return to your home or your people, but you will join the countless dead as I raze your disgusting, Christ-murdering, filthy, people from the earth. Even without Beliya'al and Mammon, I am a new god with the power of the box, and my first decree is your extinction."

Malechai rolled his eyes. "Well, turns out anyone can make a deal priest, it just takes a real man to hold to their part of the bargain."

Mal tossed the saddlebag forward. It landed with a squelch of blood and rotting meat at the priest's feet. He looked down, confused by the parcel, and used his foot to kick it open, revealing the pile of phalli within.

"What is this?"

"It's short . . . " Agrat answered for Dragan, her dark eyes glowing with a faint purple light. "Ninety-eight. I said one hundred."

"This is your deal? This is why you went through my city slaughtering everyone you met? To gather cocks for the whore?" The priest burst out in laughter.

"Baladan's dissolved," Mal answered Agrat, ignoring the priest. "I'll owe you.

Agrat's eyes narrowed, but he saw the playful smirk flit across her mouth. "You'll owe me. And I will collect that debt, Malechai ben Palache, don't you think I won't."

The priest, who had watched all of this with a smirk, shook his head. "Ah, it has been amusing, it has, but now it's over. Agrat will serve as the replacement for my toys at the entrance you murdered, and with you, I will take my time, Jew. I will visit every horror I can imagine upon you, and then I will stretch your skin out and make a new alter cover so that I may supplicate to Christ on the back of his murderers." Even in his mad dash to become a god of vile degeneracy, he still pretended at some form of faith. But before the priest could drag his blade across Agrat's throat, Mal's pistol rang out, catching the priest in the other shoulder and spinning him away from her.

"Sic em!"

Mishpat leapt over pews, barreling into the priest and dragging him to the ground.

Agrat skittered away from where the priest and golem rolled in a terrible wrestling match and ran to Mal. As she reached him, she wrapped her hands around his head and pulled him down. Pressing her lips against his, she exhaled. He was confused for a second, and then the power flooded into him. It filled him, her breath carrying with it the full might of her rage, her hurt, her strength. When she released him, she slid down his chest, and he felt invincible. He looked down at her. She looked human, no longer possessing the supernatural beauty of a succubus. But she was lovely, and even without the drawl of supernatural hooks, his heart thudded hard, looking into her dark eyes.

"Get off me, you damned mutt!" The priest's words broke the spell as the man stood holding the clay mastiff by the throat and tossed him aside. "I will make you pay for that, Jew!" An infernal green light poured from the priest's eyes as he floated above the dais. "You think by ending Baladan and Mammon to steal my strength, but it was a mere fraction of that I possess. You cannot face me and hope to prevail!" Tentacles burst from under the priest's robes, writhing tendrils of spike-lined suckers that all reached for Malechai.

Mal gently pushed Agrat aside and into a pew. "You better not have hurt my dog." Wisps of sulfur rose from his mouth as he spoke, demonic power saturating his being. He walked up the pews towards the priest. He raised his gun and pulled the trigger, firing several shots. Each bullet stopped before they reached the priest, floating in the air as if they had been fired into molasses. The priest raised his hand and lazily flicked his fingers forward. All five shots rocketed back towards Mal. The shirt, still magic, stopped three of them, but one bullet lodged in his thigh and another slammed through his shoulder. Mal cried out in pain but didn't collapse. The fortitude that Agrat had gifted him kept him up. He tossed his gun aside and charged towards the floating priest.

"Die, Jew!" the priest growled through a mouth that had lost definition in a face that was melting into something malleable and diabolic. He looked for all the world like a horrendous squid that had been forced into the shape of a man. Mal reached the dais and leapt, drawing his knife. His legs carried him further than humanly possible. He plunged the blade into the priest's shoulder as the tentacles slammed into his body, digging into his flesh. Agrat's infernal power healed his wounds, closing them as soon as they opened. But the priest was likewise unharmed. It was a stalemate between the two as they ripped into one another. Mal's scarred face twisted in hate as his eyes, dripping with purple fog, met the green distended pupils of the mad priest. Were they cursed to spend eternity locked in battle?

The only limits set on the violence they did were their own tolerances for pain. For even though he healed each suckered puncture wound, the pain was intense. The tendrils ripped not only through his flesh but through his very soul, ripping through every sense at once. Malechai roared as he stabbed into the meat, trying to sever tentacles and free himself. But for every tentacle Malechai severed, three more took its place. The priest opened his misshapen mouth, a serrated beak emerging and opening to scream a black song that sounded like the end of all things. Malechai's eyes bled as he returned the cry with his own scream of rage.

As the two empowered mortals fought, Agrat circled around the church to the twitching pile of clay and precious stones. Whispering in the secret language of creation the words that had been taught to her by Lillith, who carried the truths of beginnings down through the eons, Agrat soothed the pain of the golem and reformed it. Though her power was Malechai's to control, the secret knowledge of the world was still hers to use. And she used it to form a massive lupine humanoid from Mishpat's body. Rising from the floor, its own howl joined that of the powers battling, and it threw itself into the melee.

The priest tore Malechai away from him, using the greater reach of his tentacles to hold the enraged Mal out of knife's reach, and turned to face this new threat. He had already destroyed the golem once; it would be no issue to do it again. He hurled Malechai down, allowing him to bring the full force of his might on the clay creature.

Malechai hit the floor hard enough to rebound off the hard wood, but as he pulled himself up, he realized the priest's mistake. He couldn't beat the priest so long as he held the power of the dybbuk box. But that was a fleeting thing, a tenacious power at best. Malechai ran up the steps of the dais to the altar, ducking and weaving between the thrashing tentacles. There on the altar was a simple looking wooden box filled with human teeth. Malechai slammed the lid of the box closed and grabbed it off the altar.

The effect was immediate. All around the church, a foul wind howled, blowing out the light from the lanterns, leaving them in darkness but for the sickly green light of the priest. But that faltered. Dragan Risti screamed in pain as the power was ripped from him, his bones and skin stretching and cracking back into a human configuration as he plummeted to the floor. His head slammed into the alter as he fell, and his body bounced several times, still writhing and jerking from his unwilling transformation into a simple man. The wind continued to build, ripping curtains away from stained glass windows, which in turn shattered, letting natural sunlight stream into the building, revealing in stark contrast the depths of Risti's cruelty. The priest whimpered as he tried to push himself up and face Malechai.

For his own part, Malechai's eyes were on the terrifying half-lupine form of the golem. It was a nightmare might of earth that growled low. But Agrat moved past it and whispered "בלכ". Quickly, the creature underwent a similar metamorphosis as the priest, its body twisting and churning, flowing from one form into another until the mastiff shape had been reinstated. Agrat stepped up to Malechai, a grim smile on her face as she lifted her hand and touched his cheek. He felt the power, her power, flow from him and into her, leaving him weak-kneed and in tremendous pain.

"You owe me . . . " she whispered in his ear.

He nodded and retrieved his gun, taking the time to reload it before stepping towards the priest.

"Wait, stop, don't do this . . . you have the box, you have your precious freedom. You have conquered all the demons of hell and dismantled my church! What more could you want?" Dragan pleaded. Now powerless, with no flock to rile up, with no demons or power to put him above the simple and dirty death that awaited him, he revealed himself to be nothing but a coward. At some point, during his fall, he had pissed himself. The stench of his fresh urine mingled with the rot of death and the coppery sting of blood that had been shed in this unholy place.

"You ask what I want?" Malechai said, his scar-stretched smile widening. Behind him, Mishpat limped and Agrat crossed her arms under her breasts, neither willing to interrupt Malechai's vengeance. "I want my brother back. I want the lies you have spoken to have never been. But those . . . those are impossible. No, now all I want, priest, is to kill you."

"Kill me? That's all you want? You have the box, the entire world is at your fingertips, and I can help you achieve that. I can give you literally all of creation because I know what the demons want; I know how to control them. Spare me and you'll have everything you have ever wanted!"

Yet another degenerate seeking to make bargains with him . . .

"Agrat, excuse us, I want to have some words with the priest. Some privacy, please." Mal's voice was hoarse, sore. It hurt to speak. He looked at the succubus, his fingers idly playing across the butt of his gun.

Agrat looked like she was going to argue with him, but finally nodded and stalked out of the church, followed by the golem. She spared a backwards glance at the two men as she pushed through the doors and into the sun.

Mal turned back towards the priest.

Malechai lifted the gun from between the priest's eyes, bemused. He had no hell to fear, and of all the sins he had committed and blood he had spilled, this would be holy work in comparison. In fact, a clean death by bullet was too clean, too kind. He lowered the gun and ignored the priest's sigh of relief. He stooped down and picked up the flensing knife, the blade that Dragan had been using to torture his unwilling sacrifices. The very blade Risti had held against Agrat's throat.

Dragan's eyes were wide and panicked. "No . . . but you, you are religious! You spilled so much blood, think of the punishment you will receive from your god for your sins! Killing a priest is sure to push you over to hell. Assuage your soul of guilt!"

"You need to study your bible, Priest, for is it not said that if a thief is found, and is struck so that he dies, there shall be no guilt of bloodshed?"

Whatever response Dragan was going to make was lost in his screams as Malechai went to work. There was plenty of inspiration for bloody work hanging from the walls in the form of the priest's many victims.

CHAPTER FIFTEEN
THE REWARDS OF GOOD DEEDS

OURS LATER, Malechai pushed through the doors of the church. He was soaked in blood, but it was nothing new. He would find some place to wash before he started riding out of town. Maybe new clothes all together. The saddlebag rested on his good shoulder, though one side ·was empty now. He glanced around and was somewhat surprised to see Agrat and Mishpat waiting for him across the street, leaning against a post. He took the steps down to the road slowly, favoring his right leg, the one without the bullet in it. He didn't glance back as the flames he had set using the gas lanterns began to rise out of the windows and roared to new heights. The smell of burning wood and roasting flesh filled the late afternoon sky of Brodie.

"Wasn't sure you would still be around," he said as he approached them, patting his right thigh and calling Mishpat to his side. He walked past Agrat and took the reins, leading the horse away from the burning building.

"Well, I figured you had something for me," she responded, not moving from where she was leaning against the post.

Malechai nodded and reached into his coat. He withdrew a wad of something crumpled and bloody and tossed it to Agrat. "Figured you could make something nice of it."

Agrat unfurled the wad, revealing the whole flayed skin of Dragan Risti, peeled from the bone and muscle with patience and dedication to the craft. It flapped in the breeze like a flag celebrating the death of the mad priest. The fleshless cock fluttered uselessly, an empty tube of skin. Agrat nodded, pleased to see that Malechai had taken the time to preserve as much of the skin as he could. She glanced up from her gristly trophy and saw Mal setting the saddlebags on the horse. "Are you going back now? Returning the box and going back to your family and the Ukraine?

Mal sighed, looking over the town. He reached into his coat and pulled the box of teeth out, and turned it over in his hands. It was a damned thing, a prison, a relic of monstrous power filled with monsters of its own. Did he trust the rabbis to guard such a thing? Did he trust even Mishpat? He tucked the box back into his coat. "No, I think I'll head south. I've heard that there might be a place for people like me in Texas. I have enough gold from the dead. I could set up my own place, make my own way, maybe a little trading station. I can name it after my home."

"What? Odessa, Texas? That doesn't exactly roll off the tongue. And won't your people come looking for you, come looking for the box and for the golem?" Agrat asked, bringing up fairly good points that he no longer gave a shit about.

"They might, but truth be told, I trust myself with these more than I trust anyone else. If they have a problem, they can come looking for me . . . " He paused and grinned. "In Odessa."

Agrat rolled her eyes. "So you'll break their trust, and you'll break your promise to me as well? You still owe me one." She pushed off the post and walked towards him. "One hundred, I asked for one hundred, and you delivered ninety-nine. But I lent you all my power. Are you going to leave that debt unpaid?"

"Well, I figure you could always just let me keep mine

as a loaner, use it when you want to. I'll hold on to it the rest of the time for you." He looked down at her, feeling a little bit like a teenager who had just asked a girl to a dance.

"Are you asking me to come with you, Malechai ben Palache? To come with you solely so I can make use of you as part of our deal? You're trying to bargain your own manhood away and keep it at the same time?" she asked crossly, arching an eyebrow.

Mal sighed, his scarred face dropping to a serious expression. "Depends. Is it working?"

Agrat stood there, beautiful, fury and passion incarnate, her hands on her hips. For a moment, Malechai thought he had misjudged and she would take what she was owed and leave his corpse there in the dirt.

Finally, she laughed, a genuine laugh, and shook her head. "Texas, huh?" she asked, moving forward to put a hand on his bloody leg. "Well, let's get you cleaned up before we hit the trail."

"Yes, ma'am." He nodded before leading the horse down the road towards the saloon and her apartment.

Agrat was right, the box, the golem, even Agrat herself, would attract attention, hunters and madmen, occultists and fanatics. Even now, he was sure a bounty was being put on his head for his actions here. But he wasn't one to ever grow idle. Whoever came looking for him would find that Malechai was ready. Yes, he would be ready, and he spared no guilt or mercy for those who would seek to break his peace.

Malachai pushed open the door to the room above the saloon where Agrat made her home. The window was covered, plunging the room into darkness that belied the daytime brightness outside. Agrat started to barge past him, eager to gather her meager belongings for the trek ahead of them, but Malechai held up a hand, holding her back gently. Something else was in the room. Mal stepped forward, his dark eyes searching the darkness, his hand on the iron at his side. A sudden light, small but blinding in the near blackness, sparked to life at the end of a matchstick, revealing the haggard face of a man used to being hunted. The man brought the flame up to his face to light a cigarette, revealing burning coals for eyes and an odd symbol that had been branded under his left eye.

The intruder finally looked up, meeting Mal's hard gaze, and with a voice like the deepest pits of Sheol, the Black Magpie spoke "Got a proposition for you, Malechai."

ABOUT THE AUTHOR

John Baltisberger is an award-winning author of speculative and genre fiction that focuses on themes of body-horror, ultra-violence, and Jewish mythology. Though mostly known for his unique blend of Jewish mysticism and splatter, John defies being labeled under any one genre. His work has spanned extreme horror, urban fantasy, science fiction, cosmic horror, epic verse, and bizarro.

Beyond his writing career, John is the Publishing Editor of Madness Heart Press, a press focused on transgressive and experimental horror. He also runs the Jewish Speculative Fiction press Aggadah Try It, and the game company Madness Heart Games, where he works as the Creative Director. He lives in Austin, TX with his wife and his daughter.